# *Suped and Duped*

### *Jonas Lane*

*First edition. May 25th 2020*

*Written by JONAS LANE.*

*Published by Jonas Lane Writing Ltd.*

# Suped
# and Duped

*Jonas Lane*

*Published by Jonas Lane Writing Ltd. 2020*

# Contents

# Suped
# and Duped

## About the author

Jonas Lane is an acclaimed author and educator who is never happier than when he's telling a tall tale, whether it's to his readers or the children he teaches daily…

Jonas has written several books across a number of different genres, including the hugely popular Lord Thyme-Slipp series, regularly fusing historical fact with hysterical fiction

Although predominantly classified as a children's and YA author, Jonas Lane's books appeal to all ages, his reading audience being those that are still young at heart. Every novel Jonas has had published so far has been rated as 5-star by those who have reviewed them, young and old

In addition to writing novels, Jonas Lane is also a published poet and has written articles both locally and nationally, as well as being a former television and music critic for the Bedfordshire Times newspaper.

When not writing or teaching in school, Jonas runs his own creative writing workshops, inspiring the next generation of writers and authors.

Jonas lives in a North Bedfordshire village over the hills and faraway…

**Visit Jonas at his website**
**www.jonaslaneauthor.com**

# Foreword

Normally with my own books I don't write forewords as I like my readers to explore the story for themselves without a hint as to what may come next.

However, on this occasion, it is necessary to give some context to the tale that I tell within these pages.

*Suped and Duped* was originally going to be the short story which accompanied those written by my Young Writers' group, having spent nine weeks together looking at the superhero genre, our final week being the one where they'd finalise and submit them to me to proofread, edit and make any necessary changes before publication...

Then came lockdown and the world stopped for them and me.

Naturally, the first priority has been for everyone to keep as safe as possible which has meant that the stories the children were due to complete and submit have not happened, as have other things when Covid 19 caused us all to hit life's pause button.

But not only did it cause my time with the young writers to be put on hold, it also meant not seeing the rest of the children I teach, the school that I work in becoming a sanctuary for the children of the key workers instead.

*Staying in* has become the new *going out*, social distancing the expectation except for those who are thrown under a bus to protect the interest of others.

Amidst the fear, uncertainty and double standards I've witnessed every day since, I wrote this book. Partly as a way to maintain my own mental health but also on behalf of those who were unable to complete their own superheroic stories in or out of our clubs and schools.

It a silly little tale of about young, accidental superheroes which in the grand scheme of things counts for nothing when put against the sacrifices that the NHS, teachers, carers and other keyworkers have made to keep everyone safe no matter their colour, creed, nationality or sexuality. True superheroes of our society who have stood firm with bravery and pride despite the dangers caused by both the virus and an ineffectual government who are making it up as they go along, putting their own self, political and financial interests before the lives of countless thousands who have died or had their lives affected by their blind ignorance and arrogance.

*'A nation of heroes led by donkeys'* is the best way to describe our country today, it being the most succinct description of this country's real supervillains in our hour of need

I hope that you enjoy this book and that it provides you with a little escapism for the challenges that still lie ahead of us in the weeks and months ahead.

However, instead of leaving a review of the book as I would normally ask, please could you join a union or political party instead, one which will put the people of this great country of ours first and ensure that those who have led us blindly down these dark roads never have the opportunity to ever lie and mislead the people who entrusted them to care for us all ever again…

That would be the most superheroic act of all time…

*Jonas Lane*
*May 2020*

To my *super* young writers
Aaron Asare
Amy Rose
Bibi Kaighin
Daria-Rut Drugaci
Elisha Shaijan
Emily Kalamees
Fausta Laurinaityte
Lola Dennis
Joseph Abilash
Julia Odwrot
Kohinoor Singh
Krzysztof Buza
Lily Wooding
Lukas Saayman
Malakai Bomolo-Smith
Margot Ibbertson
Maya Maksymowicz
Mia Williams
Nathan Nahimana
Olivia Marin
Owen Ashton
Paulina Sawa
Riley Cupit
Riley Anese
Sacha Hardwick
Shakhur Nahar
Taniya Bijoy
Tom Allen

*and the children and staff of Camestone School, as well
as all those who selflessly risk their lives to care for,
protect and save the lives of others. You are all
superheroes, every last one of you.*
*Thank you*
*J.L. x*

# Chapter 1

Have you ever been caught up in an argument between two other people?

You know, when there are the three of you and two of them disagree about something or other.

Or they have an inexplicable falling out and you're caught right slap-bang in the middle of it?

In my experience, it can go one of three ways.

You pick sides, refuse to choose between them or somehow you find that you are no longer part of the three anymore.

The first option always alienates one friend which makes the situation go on even longer and you lose one of them as a friend.

Option number two is just as bad as you run the risk that the argument cannot be resolved and so you all can no longer be together as a three because two of you can't bear to be around one another any longer.

Of course, there is the final possibility – that they will find a common reason to put their differences behind them but never forget that you refused to support either of them, so they both end up ganging up on you instead!

Scenarios like this are bad enough for any teenager – they're even worse when two of your friends have superhuman powers…and you don't!

Oh, sorry, did I throw you a bit?

My bad.

Well I suppose I'd best fill you in on the detail.

You see, they weren't always super, my friends, not in the superhero sense anyway.

No, back in the day, Kai and Mez were just like any

other fourteen-year-old kids – just like me, in fact.
Boring, ordinary teenagers, living boring, ordinary lives.
Similar lives, similar interests, similar problems.
Nothing else extraordinary about us, just our friendship, which was the very best a friendship could possibly be..
We were close – tight in fact.
Little did we know what the future would soon have in store for us and how our friendship would be tested to the very limit, by circumstances way beyond our imagination and control.
We'd known each other ever since reception, being together throughout our school life, forging bonds of friendships that we thought could never be strained or broken.
How wrong we were…

Don't get me wrong, although we were so close and got along so well, we weren't total clones of each other,
far from it.
In fact, we were all polar opposites in some respects.
But it was that diversity that made our little group such incredibly fun to be a part of.
First off, there was Kai, your typical alpha male.
Tall, dark, incredibly handsome, the type of boy that all girls – and some guys – would fall head over heels in love with.
He was your typical strong, silent, brooding type, the sort of guy that you'd take to meet your parents, the one who'd turn up and run errands for his elderly neighbours.

Kai didn't have a bad bone in his body and was as straight as a die, the sort of kid that you could rely on in any crisis or emergency.

By contrast, Mez was totally the opposite to Kai in both looks and personality.

Trim and petite, she was waif-like in appearance – fragile even.

But looks can be deceiving, for Mez burned with passion and fury, being the very epitome of an underdog who never knew when she was beaten in an argument.

Which, by the way, was never.

Above all else, Mez was mischievous, with a lust for life that often got her in trouble, both at home and school.

But did she learn from her mistakes…far from it!

Once Mez had crossed a boundary, she would then go all the way to push every one she encountered as far as she could over the border with her.

But we loved her, and still do of course, Mez being the ying to Kai's yang.

Which then left me, the third wheel on our wagon.

It's often difficult to describe yourself and what you bring to the table when you have two other incredibly strong personalities to contend with.

I was labelled *the sensible one*, more like the shy, boing unconfident one if you'd have asked me.

But Kai and Mez loved having me around, so I suppose that speaks volumes for how they viewed me, as well as what they thought of my personality and character.

"AJ, we'd be totally lost without you," Kai once said to me when I questioned why they hung out with me.

"Absolutely," Mez added, "Who else is smart enough to get us out of the scrapes we get ourselvesin than you!"

That was my gift I suppose – my ability to think rationally without letting either my values or teenage sense of adventure get in the way when having to make a decision.

The right decision, more often than not.

'*Good old dependable AJ*', they called me.

Dull and predictable AJ, more like.

However, my decisiveness was a quality that I was more than a little grateful for when our worlds were Suddenly turned upside down through no real fault of our own.

When not only our friendships were put to the test, but also the lives and livelihoods of our families, friends and neighbours were put into jeopardy.

All because of an injection which came with a warning that there may be some minor after-effects.

'*Nothing to worry about*' they said, '*all perfectly normal*' the standard warning that they gave with the 3-in-1 teenage booster that all children had on reaching the age of fourteen.

You see, the teenage booster, also known as the Td/IPV vaccine, was given to us to boost protection against three separate diseases: tetanus, diphtheria and polio.

Three diseases safely managed every year thanks to breakthroughs in modern medicine preventing debilitating illness being caught by the young, previously administered safely by a single jab for many, many years in schools.

A fool-proof system for teenagers, one of those '*if it*

*ain't broke...'* procedures that world normally have resulted in a dead arm for a day or two.

*'Nothing to worry about'* nurses would say when stabbing the arms of generations of fourteen-year olds.

But that was before the medical council decided to change things, to help protect the lives of the generations to come, making one small change to the vaccine we received.

After all of the different coronavirus outbreaks that we'd had in the years before we'd reached the grand old age of fourteen, the government decided to increase our boosters, adding a fourth strain of vaccine to protect us, to immunise us against any eventually, having been arrogant to, and grossly negligent of, any health emergency in the past.

A fourth strand to go alongside the Td/IPV vaccine. Ladies and gentlemen of the jury let me introduce you to the one, the only… CoV3n13, designed to protect us against any new strain of coronavirus that may decide to raise its ugly face in future.

After the horrors of the world being locked down by the pandemic known as COVID 19, the besieged government and their medical advisers were desperate to repair the public's trust in them and not make the same devasting mistakes which turned a manageable health disaster into a national tragedy.

So as soon as the dust settled on the first great pandemic of the $21^{st}$ century, money was thrown at preventing a second one as dramatic as the first, which had ripped families, communities and, as it transpired, the whole country apart.

Therefore, when whispers started to grow of the

potential of a new strain of virus which could stunt the development of the country's youth just a few short years later, Downing Street's PR department went into full effect, announcing free vaccinations including C0V3n13 for all teenage children.

*'The saviour of the next generation'* the government's advisors and spin doctors proudly called it.

*The Witches Brew* the press nicknamed it soon afterwards.

So safe, the media announced, that only one in a hundred thousand people would notice any form of side effect of the vaccine.

Try telling that to us now.

Try telling Kai and Mez that they were being greedy, denying nearly two hundred thousand people the opportunity to experience what they did.

The super-vaccine designed to prevent them catching any super-virus did exactly the opposite.

It made my friends even more special, but in an entirely different and unexpected way...

They became *super*...

# Chapter 2

Now I know what you're thinking…

*But always in the comic books it's either a top secret experiment that's gone wrong or the protagonist is a mutant or something like that.*

*In real-life, no one simply gets super-powers, especially not from a simple, school injection.*

Well, your honour, I present to your Exhibits 1 and 2…Kai Kennedy and Mez Monroe, the newest members of the *Supers* collective.

At first, it wasn't that obvious to us that there was anything different about them.

They were still just Kai and Mez in so many ways.

But there were subtle little differences and changes that only those closest to them noticed.

Correction – subtle little differences and changes that only *I* noticed at first, mainly because I was so extremely close to them both, but not *too* close in seeing them for every single minute of every single day as your parents would do, often missing things that those a little removed immediately notice when next they meet.

For example, Kai seemingly became taller, more toned and buff overnight!

Like, literally.

He'd always been fit to look at, but this was like Adonis-level fit.

It was as though his body had been chiselled out of a single piece of granite.

Normally, they say that if you can *'pinch more than an inch'* then you're overweight.

Well, that wasn't the case with Kai.

Not only couldn't your find a spare inch of flesh to squeeze between your fingertips normally, now you'd struggle to pinch *any* of him.

It was as though his skin had turned to lycra, stretched to its absolutelimit over a frame where every muscle and sinew was taut and tightened to its maximum capacity.

Both Mez and I immediately noticed these physical changes in him, it's hard not to notice someone as gorgeous as Kai becoming even more attractive.

However, Kai himself seemed totally obvious to his new god-like physique, casually brushing off any comment or compliment made to him, of which there were many.

Mez and I never said anything of course.

It was always an unspoken and unwritten rule then between the three of us that we wouldn't let any feelings get in the way of our

friendship as once you've dated someone who was a friend, then you can never go back to how things were when your romantic relationship comes to an end.

But having someone looking as fit as Kai did made it hard to keep that rule, concentrating on the things that had made the three of us such a tight unit in the first place.

And that worked for a while…until I noticed that Mez had changed physically too.

Not in the normal way that most teenage girls do.

No, this was different.

This was…unusual, to say the very least.

As I've already mentioned, Mez was delicate looking and had a waif-like appearance, not being what most

ill-informed people class as *'classically beautiful'*.
Like, what is nowadays?

No, Mez was pretty – pretty cute if you honestly ask me!

However, almost overnight, she because *so* damned cute! It was as though someone had flicked a switch on a cute-magnet, one which immediately attracted everyone to her.

Actually, that's quite a good way of describing it…Mez became *magnetic*!

It didn't matter where we were, or what we were doing, guys and girls were suddenly drawn to her, almost hitting on her at every opportunity.

This was an entirely new experience to Mez who'd only ever really fancied one boy – Kai – and had held off asking anyone else out on dates as she couldn't find anyone who could compare to him.

But now, she could take her pick of the endless queue of suitors who'd suddenly appeared out of nowhere, asking Mez for her number, or giving her theirs without request.

Often, there'd be just the invitation of a drink, or the old favourite chat up line *'is this seat taken?'* those making the request seemingly oblivious to the presence of Kai and me.

Still, once we'd managed to cope with the gawping looks that Kai drew and fended off the advances of those besotted with Mez, it was still just the three of us as always.

Best friends forever, together, as always, morning, noon and night!

At first, we put it all down to the adolescence god playing its malevolent tricks on us, like it did when our growing pains caused us to, inexplicably, crash into everyday household items and objects that we ordinarily would have navigated around blindfolded the day prior, so familiar were we all with layouts of our respective homes.

*Puberty do your worst*, we thought, *nothing you do will get on the way of real friendship.*

And had it just been just physical differences, then we probably wouldn't have given the changes that had happened to our little group a second thought.

However, that was before Kai and Mez seemed to evolve for a second time, a non-physical change that dramatically altered he world around them, bringing them into conflict with friends, family and those in authority.

But, more importantly, it threatened to destroy the sanctity and safety of our little gang of three.

Again, it was Kai who first started to display the early signs that things were happening, changes that he couldn't quite explain or fully understand.

Kai had always been an honest and well-mannered boy, one who had been taught from an early age the difference between good and bad, right and wrong, treating others how he wished to be treated himself – fairly, with decency and respect (where respect was also given back, of course).

However, after the C0V3n13 jab, Kai's internal moral compass was heightened, almost fixed in one permanent direction – dead straight.

Things that his laconic nature would have normally shrugged off previously became major points of contention for him, lambasting people for dropping litter, reminding people of their manners when saying *'please'* or *'thank you'*.

Randomly shouting after people if they had not noticed something that he had done out of courtesy or *shushing* people loudly in the cinema if they were talking or using their mobile phone – even before the movie had started.

And if they dared eat their popcorn too loudly, Kai would shoot them a withering look which would cause them to think again about how hungry they really were.

Occasionally, somebody would turn to respond or hurl abuse at Kai.

However, one look at his frame – now a ridiculous six foot five for a fourteen-year-old – was more than enough to silence any popcorn filled rebellion which they may have initial felt.

Except for this one occasion which only served to harden Kai's values and beliefs, inadvertently setting him out on a path that he would never have previously thought to travel, prior to CoV3n13.

It was just the two of us for a change, Mez being on something that neither one of us had ever truly expected – a date.

A real honest-to-goodness date!

After the initial shock and disbelief, Kai and I had come around to the idea and, having resisted the urge to follow her to check out her new secret admirer, we had instead gone into the city to grab the biggest, juiciest burger that we could lay our hands – and teeth – on.

This carnivorous banquet we would never have been able to indulge in had our overzealous vegan friend been with us.

We were both stood in the queue, waiting to collect our order – Kai having supersized everything by the power of three – when we spotted a group of lads bothering a girl who was eating alone.

Kai held a watching brief as she tried to fend off the unwanted attention of the boys, all of whom we knew, having walked past them as they sat through sixth form detention on a weekly basis.

They were the worst of the worst and everyone who wasn't a friend or associate gave them an extremely wide berth both in and out of school, hoping to avoid any form of unwarranted interaction with them.

Just as the girl we watched was apparently and desperately trying to do.

Kai and I both recognised that she was also from our school, probably a couple of years above us, and was definitely someone who didn't want to be associated with these particularly undesirable school colleagues.

But this reluctance to engage with them did little to dissuade the sixth formers from disturbing her, ruffling her hair, stealing her fries and slurping her drink, as well as generally making her feel uneasy, threatened and increasingly uncomfortable.

I watched Kai bristle, struggling to contain his keenly honed and now highly-increased sense of social justice as he looked on.

One of the lads turned and sneered at him contemptuously.

"What you staring at bro?"

"You," Kai replied.

I placed my hand on his chest, feeling it seem to expand and contract, like a coiled spring as he stared down the youth who spat on the floor from the table he sat upon.

"I see," the youth sneered, slipping into the seat beside the girl, wrapping an arm around her shoulders before planting a kiss against her cheek as she recoiled from him.

"You like what you see?"

"No."

"Then come over here and discuss it with me and my friends," the youth replied, as his three friends turned to fix Kai in their sights, their laughing faces now cold and hard as their dead eyes stared at him.

"Kai," I began to whisper, "there are too m-"

But the words had barely left my lips as Kai moved towards them, the speed with which he travelled causing the restaurant's customers to lose napkins, cups and trays as he swept towards the four youths. If his movements caught me unawares, they came as a total surprise to the sixth formers as Kai quickly closed in on them.

One heard the bones in his fist shatter as they came into contact with Kai's jaw, as another launched himself onto Kai's back, only to find himself propelled through the air as Kai span around to fend off a third assailant, a palm thrust against the youth's chest sending him sliding across the restaurant floor as the deputy manager announced that our order was ready.

This left Kai facing the youth who had taunted him, his arm still around the girl's shoulders but his air of confidence having evaporated somewhat.

"Let go of her," Kai said, his voice hardly a whisper as a metallic *click* echoed in the silence.

"Make me," the youth replied, the knife that he held a

matter of inches away from the girl's face.

So Kai did…

You'd have thought that the restaurant owner would have been grateful for someone intervening and stopping a potentially life-threatening situation from occurring.

But oh no…

To the shouts of *'Look what you've done! Get out!'* Kai and I fled, the girl wordlessly mouthing her thanks as she looked down at the sixth former writing in agony at her feet, his arms tied together in a perfect knot…

We legged it down the high street as fast as our legs would carry us…

No – let me rephrase that…

We legged it down the high street as fast as *Kai's* legs would carry *us!*

You see, once out the door, Kai took off…

Literally.

By the time I'd broken into a run, Kai had disappeared, the air seeming to trail behind him, blurring in his wake.

But no sooner had I realised the fact than Kai was back, lifting me up like I was weightless, swinging me onto his back with no effort at all as he raced off again.

It was only when we stopped in the woods that looked over our home city – making the half-hour car journey on foot in less than five minutes flat – that we fully began to realise just what Kai had done.

"Dude!" I gasped, "What the?"

"I know," Kai calmly replied, without even a hint of a single bead of sweat dampening his brow, "crazy, huh?"

"Is that it? Is that all you have to say?"

Kai shrugged his shoulders as though his actions had been nothing out of the ordinary, before a huge grin broke across his face. "Cool, innit?"

We both burst out into hysterical laughter, relieved that we'd avoided a potentially deadly situation.

But, mixed within it was the adrenalin rush we felt at discovering that Kai now seemed to possess superhuman strength and speed.

"What do you think has happened to you, Kai?"

"Dunno."

"What are you gonna do about it?

"Not sure."

Typical Kai, his actions again far speaking louder than his words ever did.

We sat there silently, looking back at the city, flashing blue lights in the distance no doubt attending the scene we had left so rapidly.

It was a good minute or three before either one of us spoke again and when we did, it was Kai who confirmed what we were both secretly thinking.

"We cannot tell anyone about this, AJ," he said, "not even Mez."

# Chapter 3

Little did we know at that time, but almost to the very same second that we'd run into difficulties in the burger joint, Mez herself was having something of a revelation.

Not to the same extent that Kai had – not at that point, anywhere – but one which would send her rapidly following a similar path to the one that Kai had inadvertently paved for them both.

You see, Mez's mystery admirer turned out to be a boy called Leon who'd hit on her when she'd gone to the cinema earlier that week.

Mez had found herself laughing at his jokes as they stood in line waiting for the nacho machine to spit out their respective orders.

She was also intrigued by the way he spoke, no doubt the product of one of the two private schools in Meggerlithick that she could only dream of attending. But, more importantly, Mez thought had that Leon was quite cute, causing her to flush a little despite herself.

It was the first time she could recall anyone making her blush since she first met Kai.

It was also the first time that she'd shown any interest in anyone other than Kai as well.

So when Leon asked her whether she'd like to catch a film with him sometime, Mez was stunned and had somewhat surprised herself by answering *'yes'* almost immediately.

And so it was that as Kai and I were in our own version of *Assault of Burger Bar 13*, Mez was sitting down to watch the latest animated must-see movie with Leon, having been chauffeur driven there by his family's driver.

Yep – you heard right.

Leon's family had their own *private* driver.

At first, Mez thought it rather quaint and old fashioned that Leon insisted on paying for the cinema ticket, along with her coke and veggie corn dog, resisting the urge to *'go Dutch'* as she did whenever the three of us went anywhere.

And although she felt a little uncomfortable when Leon said that she could order anything off the menu at the pizzeria straight after the film, Mez reluctantly accepted the offer, knowing full well that she'd never have been able to pay half of the bill anyway.

No, it wasn't the fact that Leon was filthy rich and didn't mind showing off his wealth to her that got Mez's goat up, it was the way that he had generally treated people on their one and only date.

A single, unforgettable date which triggered a metabolic change in Mez as significant and dramatic as the one which I'd witnessed happen to Kai but totally different in how it altered her, both physically and psychologically.

Initially, Mez had bitten her tongue when Leon had failed to thank either attendant at the cinema who had served him his tickets or snacks before the movie, initially putting it down to absent-mindedness due to the excitement of being out on a date with her.

She'd even given him the benefit of the doubt when he distractedly failed to acknowledge the waitress in the pizzeria, uttering a dismissive *'the usual'* when asked for his order, the distain with which he made the remark - as well as the resigned look on the young girl's face – implying that he was a regular customer and that such arrogant behaviour was not unusual. However, it was during the course of the meal that Leon's conceited belief that it was his God-given right to look down on all he met which caused Mez's blood to boil, both physically and metaphorically. Having rudely summoned the poor waitress, berating her for the length of time it was taking for their starters, Leon then launched into a tirade of abuse, belittling the poor girl with every word uttered.

"It's no wonder that people like you have to work in places like this," he sneered, "you have neither the intellect nor the initiative to aspire to anything more."

"Leon," Mez had gently chided at first, quelling the anger she felt rising within her, "it's not her fault that the starters are late."

"No, you're probably right," Leon had smiled, "it's the fault of the parents who gave breath to her in the first place. You need a licence to own a television but can have a child without one!"

"I'm sorry, Mr Greville," the waitress replied, looking at Mez hoping that she would intervene on her behalf. Which, being the girl that I know and love Mez did.

"Yeah, Leon, why don't you give the girl a brea…"

But before she could complete her sentence, Mez stopped, recalling one particular word the waitress had said, totally failing to hear the torrent of abuse that Leon began launching at the young girl.

*Greville…Leon Greville…Greville Brothers…*

"I'm sorry," Mez had blurted out, stopping Leon mid-rant, 'but did you say that your surname was Greville?"

"What?" Leon had said abruptly, the mask he wore

when enticing a date out of Mez now fully slipping, revealing his true ugly nature, "What of it?"

Mez shook her head as the waitress took the opportunity to escape Leon's tirade, a wry smile now playing on her lips.

"Nothing. Just reminded me of the department store in city that we used to shop in, that's all.

Leon smiled proudly. "House of Greville. One of my family's many local business interests. At least, it used to be."

Mez felt something twist inside her.

At first she thought it was a knot in her stomach, but soon realised that it was something else that she felt.

Something deeper.

Something more intense.

An electricity now coursed through her body, tiny explosive charges seeming to detonate at the end of every nerve, making multiple, instantaneous connections with every synapse in her central nervous system.

She recalled vividly, as though it were only yesterday, the moment, several years earlier, that her parents were made redundant by the store's abrupt and sudden closure right at the start of the COVID 19 crisis, before the government guaranteed all workers full pay, forcing a thousand additional job seekers onto the market into a city scarce in employment opportunities as it already was.

As Leon had said, the Greville family had their fingers in so many pies in and around the city, both in the business and political communities.

No matter what the organisation or institution was in Meggerlithick, there was always seemed to be a familial link to the Grevilles either by direct bloodline through marriage or by simply being '*a friend of the Greville family*'.

To many, this effectively put them above the law, Meggerlithick's first family, beingone who could make or break you by who and what they knew.

They could have easily absorbed the closure of the department store with the wealth that the family already possessed but chose to let it die an unnatural death itself to suit their own political and financial purposes, needs and desires.

The Grevilles could easily have offered to re-employ those made redundant in some capacity elsewhere within their network of business organisations and enterprises, but had presented no alternative job opportunities nor financial recompense to those worse affected by the closure of the store and their subsequent loss of regular income.

Mez now relived the moment the bailiffs had arrived early one cold January morning and evicted her family from their home, neither her father nor her mother able to keep up the mortgage payments on the only property that the then eight-year-old Mez had ever called home.

A mortgage brokered and held by the First Bank of Meggerlithick, owned exclusively by the Greville family, no less.

Mez shuddered as she recalled the moment that the police had arrived to tell her mother that they'd found someone matching her father's description and could she accompany them to help confirm that it was her husband,

And then she raged as Mez realised that the boy who

sat across the table smirking at her was from the same family whose store initially closing had destroyed her once, happy family, placing her mum and her into a social system that was neither social nor cared for them.

*Steady, Mez,* she thought to herself, the anger she felt burning its way through every single fibre of her being, *you can't blame Leon for what his family did to yours. He's probably perfectly innocent in all this.* And for a few minutes, the volcano of rage that was threatening to erupt from deep within her was quelled, Mez quickly regaining her composure as the red mist slowly subsided, allowing her to calmly look at Leon once again.

Perhaps if Leon had changed the subject there and then, then there may have been a chance that whatever lay dormant in Mez's DNA would have stayed that way.

Dormant.

Maybe.

But fate has a habit of the finding the path that it will lead you on and today it was determined to change Mez and her destiny forever.

"Yes," Leon had smirked, "were it not for that pathetic excuse for a store closing, my family would not have quite the wealth or political foothold in Meggerlithick it still possesses today and we would not be here, doing this."

Mez frowned, a dozen other versions of her babbling their opinions in her head – questioning, challenging, dissecting, every word which now came out of Leon's mouth.

"How so?"

Leon grinned. "Although the store was still turning a tidy little profit, its central location was far more valuable to our future plans for the city. It was the final piece in our property development jigsaw, the one last stumbling block in completing the grand design for Meggerlithick.. Without that site being demolished, the redevelopment scheme that we arranged, partnering with foreign investors and major construction companies, would have come crashing down around our ears. We simply just had to wait until we could make those fools who worked for an offer that they couldn't refuse, especially as the pandemic was taking hold so quickly.."

Mez felt her body ignite again. "So you didn't have to close the store then?"

"God no!" Leon laughed, "If we held off closing the store a little longer, we could have probably received a bailout from our friends in the government and Greville Brothers would probably still be around now. No, the real act of genius was in getting those who were entitled to their full redundancy packages to accept just 10% of what we would have owed to them, convincing them that if they pushed for the full amount they were due, then the company would fold entirely and that they'd lose it all! Like I said, genius, huh?"

A red mist now seemed to descend across Mez's eyes as she slowly processed Leon's words, just as the waitress returned, carrying food for one of the other tables nearby.

"Any sign of our starters yet, love?" Leon barked.

"I'll go chase it up as soon as I serve this table their spaghetti," the poor girl replied.

"You're lucky that you're not wearing that spaghetti," Mez said, her pupils suddenly dilating, the colour fading out of her vision, everything fading to grey. All except the waitress, who seemed to become brighter and more vibrant as her eyes locked onto Mez's

*You'd like him to wear it though, wouldn't you,* Mez thought.

*More than anything* came the wordless reply.

*Then do it,* Mez urged, Leon oblivious to the silent conversation that the two girls were having before the waitress calmly and deliberately emptied the contents of the large bowl she held, pouring it over Leon's head.

He screamed and jumped out of his seat, ranting and raving as the girl just stood and looked at him, seemingly oblivious as to her actions.

*Tell her you deserved it,* Mez smiled, *tell her not to worry about dinner and could we have the bill.*

"I deserved that," Leon replied, his voice muted into a strange, monotonous tone, "could we get the bill please."

Mez felt a surge of energy fill her as she watched the waitress smile and then nod as she turned and headed to the till, Leon sat opposite, the pasta hanging from his head like limp, red dreadlocks, totally unaware as to where he was or what had happened to him.

*I don't know how I've done this,* Mez smiled, a devilish grin playing on her lips, *but I like it!*

The waitress returned with the card reader, offering it to Leon, who passively inserted his card and typed in his pin number.

*Make sure you give her a tip,* Mez suggested to him,

*a really big tip after being such an ass!*
*Sure thing,* Leon silently replied, taking the machine from the girl, *do you think a thousand pounds should cover it?*
*At the very least!*
*No, you're right,* Leon replied, typing the *9* digit four times on the keypad before handing the card reader back to the waitress…

"What did the waitress say?" I asked Mez when she retold me the whole story over Skype that night, her face more alert and alive than I had ever seen it before.
"She just asked us if we would like to box up our order as a takeaway instead!" Mez laughed, "I tell you AJ, it was so bizarre. I could control everything just by simply thinking it."
"So are you telling me that you're telepathic all of a sudden?" I asked, scarcely believing that a second friend had experienced such a life-changing transformation in such an incredibly short space of time.
Mez shook her head. "I wouldn't call it telepathy as I can't seem to be able read their minds – yet. No, it's as though I can captivate them, taking control of their thoughts. I've somehow seemed to have developed the power of suggestion and can make them do whatever I want!!"
"Oh god," I moaned, "does that mean you're always going to try to get your own way now?"
Mez shrugged. "I'm not altogether certain. Tried it on my parents when I got home."
"And?"

"Nothing," Mez replied, "not even a hint that they could hear what I was thinking."

"Do you think it was a one off then?" I asked, already knowing what my friend's answer was going to be.

"No, I definitely felt something, I've just got to work out how to use it. But can I ask a favour, AJ?"

"Name it," I replied, half-knowing what it was likely going to be.

"Don't breathe a word of this to Kai. Knowing him, he's bound to disapprove."

# Chapter 4

I kept my word to the both of them as I'd promised,
hoping to keep things as normal moving forward.
Well, as normal as it could possibly be now having
two friends who were superhuman, that is.
However, the next time the three of us met up,
things were a little bit awkward to say the least.
"So, what've you been up to then Mez?"
"Nothing…why do you ask Kai?"
"Oh, I was just curious, that's all."
"Who's been talking? Have you said something AJ?"
"Of course not, Mez," I replied, hoping that my face
wouldn't betray the secret that we shared, the secret
that I was struggling to keep.
"What does AJ know that I don't?" Kai asked, a deep
frown now furrowing his brow as he wondered
whether the trust he'd placed in me was misguided or
not.
"Nothing," Mez replied, a little too sharply to not be
bothered, "Lord knows, she can't keep a secret even
if she had to."
"Is that so, AJ?" Kai asked, his eyes staring at me a
little too intently.
"No, it's not as well you know!" I replied.
Mistake.
Mez was onto it like a shot.
"How would Kai know how good you are at keeping
something to yourself, unless you are of course!" Mez
asked, staring at me intently.
I could feel her probe my mind, only for the sensation
to suddenly stop as Kai stepped between us, somehow
blocking Mez's new powers of suggestion.

"What's gotten into you, Mez? You're acting well-weird."

Mez drew herself up to her full height, all five feet three of her, and stared up at Kai.

I could tell by the way that her face was flushing that she was trying to use her newly-discovered skills to bend Kai around to her way of thinking.

But seeing the devilish look she wore turn to one of utter frustration, it was obvious that she was unable to penetrate Kai's steely exterior.

"I could ask you the very same question, Kai," Mez replied, folding her arms defiantly, "you're more of a closed book now than ever before."

She sat back down on one of the beanbags in my room as Kai still stood, staring her down as he protected me from her accusations – and his own secret of course.

*It's all gonna kick off in a minute,* I remember thinking to myself as Kai eventually sat, still eyeing Mez suspiciously.

There the three of us sat, without exchanging a word or a glance for what seemed like an absolute eternity.

Nothing had directly happened between us.

But since C0V3n13, there was now definitely something in between us.

The easiness we normally felt when together was no longer there.

We were somehow drifting apart.

It was as though Kai and Mez were now so magnetic and similar that they repelled each other instead of being attracted to the things that they'd once both shared in common.

*God, this is awkward,* I thought, desperately trying to

think of something to say or do to break the ice that had frozen over the three of us.

However, it was left to Mez to put a premature end to proceedings.

"I'd love to sit here and chat," she said sarcastically, "but I've *stuff* to do. Laters."

"Laters," I replied, looking at Kai, who merely nodded his silent goodbye.

Awkwardly, I walked downstairs to see Mez out.

As we stood at the door, she turned and whispered to me.

"You free after school later this week, AJ?"

"Um…I think so," I replied, slightly caught on the backfoot by the question.

"Good," Mez smiled as she made her way down the path towards my front gate, "I've been thinking about what's happened to me. Could do with your opinion in things."

"OK," I replied, "I'll see what day works best for Kai."

"No…don't!" Mez said firmly, "The less he knows about what's happening, the better. Besides, there's definitely something a little *off* about him at the moment."

*That's rich,* I thought, waving her off, Mez seeming to hover above the ground slightly as she skipped off down the street.

I closed the door and went back upstairs to find Kai now stood at my window, staring out of it intently as Mez slowly disappeared from view.

"I hate to say it, but I'm glad she's gone. There was a really odd vibe here tonight," Kai said moodily, quickly changing the subject, "Anyway, I need your help. Just you, mind. I can't ask Mez, especially as she seems kinda *off* at the moment...."

Suddenly, I began to laugh uncontrollably, causing Kai to look at me strangely.

"What's so funny?"

"Nothing," I eventually replied, managing to quickly recompose myself, "so how can I help?"

Kai paused for a moment, as though sizing up whether I was telling the truth or not before eventually continuing.

"Are you free one night after school this week....?"


Now, I have few qualities that I am proud of.

For example, I can make my eyes 'walk', controlling them so that it appears that they move independently of one another from one side of my face to another

I can also roll my tongue, which has no practical benefits other than the fact it freaks people out and looks pretty cool.

Some might say that my greatest quality is my speed of thought and quick wit which has dug me and my friends out of the odd scrape or two during the fourteen tender years I've walked on this planet.

But were you to ask those that know me best whether you would put the name '*AJ Sipowicz*' and the phrase '*possesses a keen sense of fashion*' together in the same sentence, then I can say with great certainty that none would offer to do so.

Yet this is what Kai expected of me as we walked down the High Street later that week.

"You seriously want me to help you clothes shop?" I asked as the two of us strode along the damp pavement, my voice raised so as to be heard above the deafening roar of the busy traffic around us.

"Uh-huh," Kai replied.

"But you always look so damned sharp in whatever you normally wear, so how could I even possibly help?"

As we stopped, waiting to cross the road, Kai looked at me without a hint of humour in his face.

"Because I want to look *different*."

"So you fancy a change in style then," I replied as we quickly made our way in between the cars travelling in both directions, too impatient to wait for the pedestrian lights to change, advising us when it was now safe to cross.

"Not exactly," Kai replied as we walked down the alley that led to a small cluster of independent shops that were known only to a select few.

Diverse and independent specialist shops, one of which was the last place that I would have ever expected to find my clean-cut, super-smooth friend browse in.

"The Goth Shop!" I gasped as Kai made to open the door, "Seriously?"

Kai nodded, allowing the door to close again.

"Absolutely."

"I'm sorry, but I just can't see you pulling off the vampiric-poet look, Kai!" I laughed.

My friend then laughed despite himself.

"Ordinarily, no," Kai smiled as he again opened the door and stepped into the shop, "however, I need a look so totally at odds with the one that people would normally associate with me."

I quickly followed him into the Goth Shop, past the multi-pierced and tattooed face of the shop assistant who was pouring over a music magazine at the counter.

"Why ever would you want to look different, Kai?" I asked as he rifled through a rail of long, leather coats that hung at the back of the shop.

Kai pulled a particularly militaristic looking one out and held it against him as he looked in the mirror behind where I stood. He handed me the hanger as he put it on, the coat almost attaching itself to his body, seeming to become a second skin, as Kai flexed his arms in it before suddenly doing a roundhouse kick, much to my bemusement.

"Because I don't want anyone to recognise me when I take to the streets at night," Kai said nodding to the *mirror-Kai* who nodded his approval back.

"Take to the streets?" I asked as Kai picked up a rivetted, leather mask and held it to his face, it concealing the lower half of it, the single silver skull that adorned it resting on the bridge of his nose.

It immediately brought back several unwanted memories of when all of us in school had to wear masks in school for health and safety reasons.

"What do you think?" he asked, his voice slightly muffled by the material that covered his mouth. I chose to ignore the question.

"Take to the streets, Kai?" I repeated, remembering what he'd previously said, "What the hell are you talking about?"

Kai shrugged, removed the mask and the coat and, grabbing a pair of studded gloves made his way to the counter. "I'll tell you outside."

Seeing him not bat an eyelid at spending £500 to look like a fading rock star was almost as painful as the suspense Kai was keeping me in as we stood outside the shop again, the rain now falling more heavily than before.

I looked at him again, frowning, my expression leaving him in no doubt that I was still wanting for an answer to my earlier question.

Kai grinned. "Let's get a coffee – my treat. Then I can tell you all about my plans to clean this city up once and for all."

I was still processing Kai's revelation that he wanted to use his newly found powers to rid our city of the undesirable element that had grown over the past few years when Mez text me to ask whether I'd like to go the new gelato restaurant the following Saturday.

Of course having a sweeter than average tooth meant that I was never going to say no, especially as it would be a welcome distraction from the plans that Kai had so enthusiastically shared with me just an hour earlier.

"You want to become a crime-fighter?"

"Yep," Kai replied.

"A vigilante?"

"Uh-huh."

"A suburban superhero?"

"That's right."

"Kai, in case you hadn't noticed, this is the west of England, not Manhattan."

"Meaning?"

"Meaning, name me a Great British superhero."

"Erm…"

I knew that I had him there and then.

I mean, when you think *superhero*, you think Marvel

and DC, not Marks and Spencer.

But as I watched him doubt his reasons momentarily, I felt a mixture of pride, fear and guilt battling for supremacy with one another.

Pride in the fact that my friend wanted to do something worthwhile with the gift that he'd somehow accidentally inherited.

Fear from the knowledge that Kai was prepared to put himself in harm's way when confronting a whole host of dangerous and unsavoury characters who'd chosen our city as a base for their vile and detestable operations, capitalising on its proximity to several major motorways, as well as two ports and a small, international airport.

An instant transport network to peddle their filth in and out of the city.

However, guilt was the emotion that was winning its battle for my attention.

Guilt from not being able to dissuade him.

Guilt from knowing that I didn't have the physical strength to help him.

Guilt from the fact that he had powers that I envied and yearned for.

But most of all, guilt from the knowledge that if I'd have inherited his gift then there wasn't a cat-in-hell's chance that I would even go near one of the no-go areas that had increased in the city late at night.

So it came as some relief to me that I was going to meet Mez for an ice cream the following Saturday afternoon.

As I got off the bus opposite *Ice 'n' Easy*, my friend *Mr Guilt* first tapped me on the shoulder, before slapping me squarely across the face.

*Don't tell Mez about Kai,* it whispered.

"I won't," I mumbled as I waited to cross the road, seeing Mez already sat in one of the booths, a broad grin filling her face as she waved at me.

*You swear?*

"Swear down," I whispered to myself, repeating the words I said to Kai when he made me promise not to breathe a word of his plans to anyone.

Plans that he aimed to put into place the very same day I dashed between the vehicles, taking my life in my own hands for a second time in quick succession, to meet Mez.

"Hey," I said cheerily as I slid into the booth, smiling at my friend now sat across the table from me.

"Hey, AJ," Mez smiled, adding, "I ordered us both a Caramel Popcorn shake. That good with you?"

"Absolutely," I smiled as I picked up the huge, saccharine-filled dessert menu and pondered what would give me the best simultaneous sugar-hit and brain-freeze, grateful for a little normality, having spent the past few evenings with my soon-to-be-superhero friend.

Whilst I sat in caramel-popcorny bliss, having placed my order, *Mr Guilt* quietly began to snigger in my ear as I looked at Mez who was blissfully unaware of Kai's plans, nor my part in the subterfuge.

As she stared at me, I prepared myself to turn away from her as Mez's eyes burned into mine, trying to seek out the answers that lay behind them, secrets deeply burrowed away from her mind's reach.

This feeling was made worst by knowing that Mez had also evolved and that whatever had happened to Kai must have also now happened – in part – to her.

As we stood eating the large ice-creams we'd just been served, I knew that it was only a matter of time before she teased out the answers that her piercing orbs sought to tear from my guilt-ridden soul.

Yet, as we ate, the smile that played on her lips faded a little, as though frozen by the ice-cream itself.

Now I don't know about you, but when someone stares at me for an inordinate amount of time, a number of questions immediately spring to mind…

*What are they staring at…?*

*Have I got something stuck on my face…?*

*Do they fancy me…?*

*Are they secretly plotting to kill me then…?*

Unable to contain my curiosity any further, I decided to broach the subject with Mez as subtly as possible, without arousing any further suspicion…

"What?"

Mez smiled and took another spoonful of the multi-coloured ice-cream that now melted over the edge of her glass dish.

"Nothing."

"Oh, there must be something, Mez, there always is!"

"Oh, you know me so well!" Mez laughed, adding, "I was just thinking that there's something different about you."

"Me?"

"Yeah. You seem…oh, I dunno, more assured of yourself, more confident in your own skin even."

This came as a total shock to me as inside my stomach was churning like waves slamming against the rocks during a storm.

"Do I?"

"Uh-huh," Mez nodded, taking another huge bite of

her ice-cream, "there's something somewhat enigmatic and mysterious about you today. I can't quite put my finger on it."

We sat there for a couple of minutes as the young waiter, dressed from head to foot in red pinstripes, closely resembling a walking deckchair, presented us with the bill.

Mez picked it up, looked at it and then, tilting her head to one side, looked deeply into the waiter's eyes as she handed the bill back to him.

"They're on the house!" the young lad suddenly said.

Mez smiled. "Why, thank you ever so much!"

"Oh, don't mention it!" the waiter replied, "It's my pleasure! I do hope you and your friend come again soon."

And that's when I realised what Mez meant by me being *mysterious and enigmatic...*

Even with her new powers of suggestion, she was unable to read or bend me to her way of thinking, unlike the poor young waiter who'd served us.

Knowing that, I immediately relaxed, knowing that Kai's secret was safe with me...

For the time being at least.

We grabbed our coats, slid out from the booth and made our way for the exit, but not before I'd secretly slipped some money under my plate on the table so that the young waiter wasn't out of pocket.

"So, what do you fancy doing now?" I asked, catching up with Mez as the bell on the door chimed behind us as we left the ice cream parlour.

"Fancy going clothes shopping, AJ?" Mez asked, adding, "I've an idea that I'd like to run past you...but don't breathe word of it to Kai!"

# Chapter 5

I felt an immediate sense of déjà vu as Mez and I trawled up and down the High Street, my friend mischievously sharing with me how she was going to use her newly-possessed powers.

"It's like I've been given a way to put wrongs right, AJ," Mez gushed as we went into the first of her favourite fashion outlets – a charity shop whose profits funded a pet sanctuary just outside of the city. Where money was no object for Kai, Mez's family circumstances dictated that she was a regular visitor to the plethora of bargain shops and charity stores that littered the main thoroughfare of our once famed and flourishing city.

As we rifled our way through the clothes that were squashed together on the rail, the familiar stale and musky charity shop aroma wafting under her noses, Mez explained to me how she was going to put her particular gift to work for others.

But where Kai's intentions were truly noble, Mez's were borne out of revenge, the chip she carried on her shoulder growing heavier by the second.

Grabbing an old and broken full-face motor-cycle helmet off the shelf, its visor having been lost long ago, she thrust five pounds towards the shopkeeper as she continued to share her secrets with me.

"There are so many families up and down the country who are either on the poverty line or have to survive on the scraps that they are fed by the well-off, AJ," Mez said as we ducked into another charity outlet, one dedicated to helping those needing end-of-life care, "look at how many people we've passed out on the streets today alone."

It was true.

In almost every other doorway we passed, there was either someone begging for money or the unoccupied remnants of the temporary home that they'd set up in the disused shop fronts.

"So you're going to become a politician then, Mez," I laughed as she held up a tight-fitting black and orange ski-suit.

"No chance!" Mez replied, thrusting the helmet she'd bought toward me, "Hold this while I try this ski-suit on."

I took hold of the helmet as she slid back the curtain of the changing room and hid behind it.

"So, if you ain't going to be a politician then," I asked as I heard Mez struggle and swear her way out of her clothes and into the ski-suit, then what are you going to do…become a super-hero?"

I could hear my friend pause behind the curtain before continuing to fabric-wrestle the ski-suit, eventually drawing the floral patterned curtain back across the rail, grabbing the helmet from me, putting in on her head to complete her new look, it covering her face so that only the bridge of her nose and her eyes were visible to the outside world.

"Not in so many words…" Mez finally replied as she stood there, her arms thrust out to either side of her, "There! How do I look?"

"Like ook like a cross between a bumble bee and a midget power ranger!" I laughed, causing Mez to raise a middle-finger towards me.

She turned to look in the mirror of the changing room

and slowly nodded her approval.

"Cool," Mez said, her voice muffled by the helmet, the shiny surface of it causing multiple reflections back and forth between the two mirrored surfaces.

I stepped to look over her shoulder and lost myself in the multiple images that I saw of the two of us as they bounced back and forth between the reflecting surface of the helmet and the mirror.

"The effect is well trippy, Mez."

"Ain't it?"

"Yep, it's…it's, oh, what's the word?"

"Mind-blowing?"

"Nah, more than that," I replied, "like when a startled rabbit gets caught in the headlights of a car."

"Transfixed?"

I shook my head before it suddenly hit me, the way to best describe how my friend now looked to me.

"Mesmerising."

"I like that," Mez replied, "and you definitely can't tell that it's me?"

I shook my head as Mez turned to look at me, the helmet now reflecting my face back in my direction.

"AJ," she said, her voice low and menacing, "I'd like you to meet my good friend *Mesmerise*, defender of the lost, lonely, ignored and forgotten…"

As we walked back to my house, Mez repeated how wrong it was that those who had so much seemed to use it as a stick to beat over the head of those that have so little.

"All my life," Mez said as we turned the corner and began to walk up the hill which led to my house, "Mum and me have lived in fear, waiting for the next final demand letter to land on our doormat, or have hidden behind the couch when the doorbell's rung as yet another debt collector has come seeking payment. And me and mum aren't alone. There are plenty others out there who are in exactly the same sinking ship as us."

"But, Mez," I protested, "what you're suggesting ain't right. Besides, taking something that doesn't belong to you, that's just not you, is it?"

"No, it isn't," Mez smiled, "it's what *Mesmerise* is for. She's gonna be a modern-day Robin Hood! Steal from the rich to give to the poor. It's not like they're gonna miss it now, are they?"

"Who isn't going to miss it?" I asked as we approached my house, stopping abruptly on seeing Kai sat on my garden wall, a large backpack resting between his feet.

Mez baulked at the sight of him, as though physically repelled by someone who only a matter of days ago was one of her closest friends.

"The likes of *him*," she said as we slowly walked toward Kai, "Mr *I'm-Hollier-Than-Thou!*"

"What's your problem?" I whispered as we watched Kai stand, a frown as dark as a storm cloud now filling his face, "You two used to be so tight."

"He's…different," Mez grunted, "For some reason that I can't explain, I don't trust him anymore. He sets my teeth on edge just by looking at him now!"

"Trust me, the feeling's entirely mutual," Kai suddenly replied.

"How the…" I gasped, realising that there was still over 100 metres between us and him.

"That's my cue to split, I think," Mez said, hugging me, "Laters."

"Ah, leaving so soon?" Kai called sarcastically,
"What a pity!"

Mez went to reply but thought better of it as she
tapped her nose. "Not a word, remember?"

I sighed and nodded.

This was getting ridiculous.

Not only were my two BFFs no longer BFFs, pitching
me firmly into the middle of their inexplicable beef
with one another but now they were planning to have
secret identities which only I would be aware of.

It suddenly dawned on me that the *A* in *AJ* could now
easily be mistaken for Alfred, Bruce Wayne's loyal
butler.

Except I was no willing sidekick, just a teenager
struggling to make sense of what was happening to
my friends and our world.

As I trudged toward Kai, he nodded at the departing
Mez rather disdainfully.

"That's a relief," he growled, "for a minute there I
thought that she was going to be staying."

"And?"

"And what?"

"And why would that be a problem?" I asked, my
patience now so thin that it had almost worn away.

"Because no one can know what I have planned," Kai
said, following me to my front door, "especially *her.*"

That was the final straw.

"What does that mean, 'especially her?' This is
insane, you two used to be so tight!" I snapped.

"True," Kai nodded, "but this gift I've developed has
somehow given me a sixth sense."

"Meaning?"

"Meaning that somehow I can spot those who have

less than good intentions."

For once, it I who was lost for words.

Although Mez was still Mez, her moral barometer was definitely veering toward *dark and stormy,* which was in total contrast to Kai's obsessive desire to continuously point directly towards the light.

And yet somehow both my friends could also see this in one another through some unspoken understanding and knowledge.

Seeking to swiftly change the subject and avoid any further discussion on the matter, I nodded towards Kai's backpack.

"So, you got your gear in there ready for tonight?"

Kai clutched the bag to his chest and patted it proudly. "Yep, all good to go."

There we stood silently looking at one another, waiting for one of us to speak next.

As usual, it was yours truly…

"So, what are you doing here then?"

Kai smiled and looked at me expectantly. "Isn't it obvious?"

"Er…no!"

"Well, Kai Chambers is having a film night with his best friend AJ tonight…" Kai smiled.

"Is he now?"

"Totally," Kai grinned, "that way I have the perfect alibi when *The Law Lord* metes out justice on the streets of Meggerlithick this evening."

"The Law Lord? Seriously?"

Kai frowned. "What's wrong with that?"

"Is that the best you could come up with?

"I'd like to see you do better," he grunted as I continued to laugh as I opened the door to my house.

"Hey there, it's only me!" I called as I ushered him in, "Can Kai stay for dinner tonight? We've a shedload of stuff that we've got to revise and go through for school this weekend…"

# Chapter 6

As usual, Mum and Dad easily saw through my pathetic attempt at subterfuge but went along with the lie, setting a place for Kai at the table, as well as preparing my brother Matty's room for himto sleep in should he wish to stay over, as he had on countless occasions since Matty had left for uni two and a half years earlier.

After dinner, the two of us went up to my room, me switching my television on so that it blared loudly, allowing Kai and I to speak without fear of being overheard or interrupted.

"You're really going to go through with this, aren't you?" I whispered as Kai slipped off his tee-shirt to reveal his torso which resembled a finely carved example of what the perfect human form should look like.

It never bothered me normally to see my friends dress and undress before me, as Kai and Mez had done ever since we'd known one another, the way that most siblings comfortably do, but tonight I flushed despite myself, my face becoming as red as my hair.

Fortunately Kai didn't seem to notice as he slid the black turtleneck he had brought with him down over his head, smoothing it against his body as it tightly welded itself to his skin.

"Absolutely," he finally replied as he unfurled the long leather coat from his backpack, slipping one arm into it as the other retrieved the gloves and mask that he'd purchased earlier that week.

"And there's nothing I can say that will make you change your mind?"

"No, there isn't," Kai replied as he continued to put the coat on, "I can't explain it, AJ, but it's like I've been building up to this point all of my life. I just needed something to push me in the right direction." He placed the mask over his mouth and tied it behind his head, before reaching into his bag again to pull out a huge pair of black, steel toe-capped DMs. Kai placed one of his feet into the boots and lifted it up onto the bed to begin tying it.

"When I discovered these strange new abilities I have, it was a though an ignition switch flicked on inside of me. Why else do you think God suddenly gave these new gifts to me?"

I smirked despite myself.

Of course it made perfect sense for Kai to think that some divine presence had *blessed* him his powers.

He came from a devout church-going family, which meant that he'd grown up believing that everything he did was determined by his faith.

It was a subject that the three of us had decided never to discuss as friends, Mez being a committed atheist where I consider myself more of a pantheist, believing that the world and the universe itself is identical to *God.*

"What's so funny?" Kai snapped.

"Nothing," I replied, biting the inside of my cheek to make my smile disappear, "it's a nervous grin I get when I'm really anxious or nervous about someting."

A little white lie, but one borne with some truth behind it.

I was really worried about Kai and what he planned to do that night.

Although he now had the physique which Thor would

have been envious of, there was no escaping the fact that he was just a kid, one who was only a couple of months older than me.

Kai smiled, buying the lie. "I've got to do this, AJ. This city's going downhill rapidly because of the scum who own the night. It's time someone did something about them"

"That's what the police are for."

"Supposedly," Kai replied as he turned to my bedroom window, "they've made little difference though, haven't they?"

I didn't reply.

I couldn't argue with his logic.

Meggerlithick city centre at night wasn't a place that you would willingly go nowadays, unless you were looking for the illegal wares offered by the gangs who seemed to populate each dimly lit alleyway or street corner.

Another by-product of our city's earlier economic ruin coupled with the arrival of those seeking new territory to rule having left the well-patrolled and overcrowded streets of our capital, seeking out less policed parts of the country.

Kai opened my window with little effort, causing me to feel a pang of envy as I always struggled with opening it myself. He swung a leg out of it, ready to drop onto the flat surface of our garage roof a few feet below it

"Kai, please don't go!" I pleaded, "You can't do this on your own!"

"I'm not alone," Kai replied, raising his fists towards me, "I'm taking a couple of friends with me!"

"I'm being serious, Kai!"

"So am I, AJ," Kai said, winking at me, "Look, don't worry, I'll be back before you know it."
Before I could say anything else, Kai had swung his other leg out, over the window ledge and silently dropped onto our garage roof.
I rushed to the window just in time to see him effortlessly jump down from the tarmacked suface, before running off at an incredible speed, briefing catching sight of his coat trailing behind him like a cape as he disappeared into the darkness of the night...

I don't know how long I sat there, the TV blaring away – until Mum and Dad asked *us* to turn it down that is,  blissfully unaware that I sat alone in my room, my mind racing, playing out a whole series of different scenarios in my head as I worried as to what Kai was now supposedly doing.
During this time, my phone buzzed wildly.
I grabbed for it, hoping to see *Kai* flash up on my screen.
I hate to say that I felt a real sense of disappointment when Mez's name was displayed there instead...

**MEZ: Can u talk?**

I didn't feel like talking so paused, carefully thinking how to reply...

**ME: No**

Genius response, eh? Still, it wasn't enough to dissuade Mez from continuing the conversation...

**MEZ: Oh...is that cos he's still there?**

I sighed and angrily typed back without really thinking through my answer...

**ME: Kinda**

What the hell was that?
What sort of reply did I think I was going to get next...?

**MEZ: Wot do u mean 'kinda'?**

It was then that I realised just how useless I was at all of this cloak and dagger stuff, secret-squirrel stuff! But now I had also started to resent my two BFFs for putting me in such an awkward position, so I decided to be as blunt and abrupt as possible so that I could finally be able to get Mez off my back...

**ME: Can't explain now,
I'll text ya 2moro 2 explain x**

A kiss?
I signed my text off with a kiss!
That was really gonna show Mez how vexed I was feeling, but I could tell by Mez's reply that she was not best pleased with my response in any case...

**MEZ: K**

Ouch!
The sure-fire way to sign off any text, showing

enough anger without being abusive yet leaving the receiver in no doubt as to how annoyed the sender was when
signing off.

But at that point I really didn't care for Mez's bruised ego as all I could think about was Kai and what was happening to him.

I lay on my bed for what seemed like ages just staring at my phone, desperate to hear from him.

But, without consciously realising I was doing it, I automatically took matters into my own hands...

**MEZ: Hey Kai, how's it goin?**

I'd hit the send button before I even knew it as, almost immediately, a huge wave of horror washed over me like an emotional tsunami...

What if he was hidden somewhere, checking out his surroundings or *casing the joint* as they always seemed to say in one of those run-of-the-mill American detective shows when his phone begins to chirp rapidly?

Or perhaps he was just about to creep up on some up-to-no-good-doer or drug-dealer when the theme to *Doctor Who* had begun to ring loudly, announcing the arrival of my text thereby alerting them to his secret, hidden presence?

Maybe at that very moment, Kai was engaged in a life or death struggle when his phone wildly vibrates in his pocket, distracting him at a pivotal moment as a series of killer blows rain down on him.

Disgusted with my thoughtlessness and stupidity, I

tossed my phone onto the bed and slumped opposite
it, my mind in turmoil as I realised what a careless
and childish mistake I had made as I lay there, hoping
– praying – that he'd soon reply...

# Chapter 7

I don't exactly know how long I lay there before sleep somehow managed to claim me as the next thing I knew, my mum was hammering on the bedroom door as the sun weakly shone through my window the following morning.

"Come on, *spíoch*!" she laughed, "Breakfast's on the table and it's already starting to get cold!"

I sat up with a start and looked at my phone, hoping to find a reply from Kai saying that he was OK…

There was none.

Panicking, I dashed out of my bedroom and into Matty's, not even knocking first which, in hindsight, could have proved embarrassing if Kai was actually in there, in some state of naked undress.

Luckily – and unluckily given the circumstances – he wasn't, my brother's bed fully made up, looking perfect and pristine, there being not a single crease in the duvet cover to betray the fact it had been occupied at any point in the past twelve hours.

My heart and hopes sank even further as I heard my dad roar with laughter from downstairs, causing me to feel angry that he could be so happy and carefree when my heart was breaking from possibly being at my lowest point ever in my life.

In desperation, I text Kai again.

### ME: Pls let me know that u r alright?

I paused briefly at the top of the stairs, biting my lip as I slowly began to walk down them, worrying as to whether I should text again especially after my fears and doubts over my previous efforts, before I finally jabbed the *SEND* button.

"Please let him reply…please let him reply," I whispered repeatedly to myself, closing my eyes in the process as, from the dining room, the opening bars to Kai's favourite TV show began to loudly ring out, a loud vibrating sound accompanying them as it rattled against our dinner table!

"I love that show, Kai," I heard my dad say as I almost fell over myself, taking two stairs at a time in my haste to reach the dining room – where I found my best friend sat with my parents, eating breakfast as though it was the most natural thing in the world for him to be doing.

"There you are, AJ," Dad smiled as he took a sip out of his *World's Greatest Father* mug, "we were beginning to worry about you, weren't we, Kai?"

I scowled at my friend now sat opposite me, cutting the sausage which sat on his plate exactly in half before popping it into his mouth.

"You were worried about me?"

"Totally, AJ," Kai smiled as he bit into a piece of toast, "especially after you fell asleep on me last night!"

"Fell asleep on you?" I asked, doubt and confusion now battling for my attention.

"Yep, left me to watch the film all alone before I eventually took myself to bed," he smiled, adding, "you must have been really tired though as you didn't even stir when I popped my head around the door this morning to see if you wanted a cooked breakfast."

"A cooked breakfast?"

"Are you half-parrot this morning, *drogi*?" Mum

asked, "Yes, the cooked breakfast that Kai got up especially early to cook for us all."

"And what a fine breakfast it is, young man!" Dad smiled, "I'd be lucky to get a slice of toast out of AJ most days!"

"Don't mention it Mr Sipowicz," Kai smiled, "It's the least I can do in return for you putting me up last night."

"Stop standing there gawping and sit, AJ," Mum urged, "your food's going to get cold otherwise."

I looked at the plate in front of me.

Normally I'd have totally devoured the bacon, sausage, egg, beans and toast on it without much thought, but my appetite had unsurprisingly deserted, replaced by the anger and relief I felt as I looked at Kai, both emotions battling against one another.

"To be perfectly honest, I'm don't really feel in the mood for breakfast this morning," I replied.

Mum placed her hand against my forehead. "Are you feeling all right, *kochanie*?"

"Yes, AJ, it's unlike you to be off your food," Dad frowned.

I looked at Kai who continued to wolf down his food. "Just don't fancy eating much this morning, that's all."

"Ah well," Kai said, rising from his seat, sweeping the contents of my plate onto his, "*'waste not, want not!'* as I always say…I'm absolutely ravenous this morning!"

"I don't know where you put it, Kai!" Dad laughed.

"Built up quite an appetite there, dude," I said sharply, "you spend the night working out or something?"

Kai shot me a glance as though to say '*don't*' as he tucked into his second helping of breakfast as my mum turned on the radio.

"So, back to our top story," the radio announcer declared solemnly, "sources today are reporting that one of the city's most notorious drug dealers, Biffy Amitri, is in police custody this morning…"

I glanced at Kai who continued to eat, seeming to show little apparent interest in the events that were now being retold over the airwaves to the morning listeners in Meggerlithick.

"…one eye-witness reported seeing a tall and powerful figure, dressed from head-to-foot in black, take on several gang members, swatting them away like flies, before grabbing Amitri…"

By now, Kai had stopped eating and was craning his head toward the radio as the four of us sat there, listening intently to the report as it continued.

"Senior police figures are refusing to confirm or deny that Amitri was deposited at Meggerlithick Police HQ by a vigilante who simply identified himself to them as The Wardrobe…"

I almost spat out my coffee at seeing the horrified look on Kai's face, realising that his finest moment was now being stolen from him in being identified as a common piece of bedroom furniture!

He scowled at me as Mum turned the radio off and re-joined us at the table.

"It's about time someone helped to clean our streets up," Dad said, adding, "though I'm not quite sure that our mysterious saviour has properly thought through their superhero name though…"

In the days which followed, I have to admit that I

took great pleasure and delight in teasing Kai as to how his secret identity had been misheard when he'd triumphantly and breathlessly mumbled '*I am The Law Lord*' to the startled police he'd deposited his first villain to.

Unfortunately for him, the moniker *The Wardrobe* soon stuck, it being frequently used more and more in the written, broadcast and television reports as Kai continued his single-handed, one-man nocturnal campaign against crime.

Although he hated the fact that he was now crime-fighting under a different identity to the one that he'd originally intended, Kai readily admitted to me how much he enjoyed reading the newspaper headlines each time he successfully carried out his lone crusade against some low-life criminal or armed gang who he'd happened to come across on his nightly patrols…

*Narnia Business!*
*Criminals Run into the Wrong Wardrobe…*

*Moth-Balled!*
*The Wardrobe Closes Down Drug Den…*
**Door Slams Shut on Gangland Boss!**
*Infamous Villain Trapped by The Wardrobe…*

**Robbers Have Another Major Wardrobe Malfunction!**
*Mystery Superhero to the Rescue Yet Again…*

***Fake Police Informer Recaptured***
*The Lying Snitch Canned by the Wardrobe…*

It was now becoming harder and harder at school to keep his secret as everyone we knew was talking about *The Wardrobe*, speculating on who he was, or spreading some tall tale or fake news story to garner favour with their friends...

*"I've heard that he shoots laser beams out of his eyes and farts lightning bolts at his victims..."*

*"My dad's a taxi driver and is hired to drive his getaway vehicle but is sworn to secrecy as to who he is..."*

*"The Wardrobe is the ghost of a dead launderette worker who used to launder money for the mob and has come back to wreak his revenge after they murdered him..."*

*"He asked me to help him once, but I was too busy doing my hair that night..."*

*"There's a girl who works down our chip shop who swears she's The Wardrobe..."*

Everybody, it seemed to Kai and me, were fascinated by the fact that we had our very own superhero in Meggerlithick to idolise and fantasise about...

Everyone that is, except Mez...

Mez didn't just feign disinterest.

Ono, she positively refused to engage in any form of positive dialogue involving Meggerlithick's new celebrity superhero.

This indifference I tolerated mainly due to the fact that there seemed to be a slight improvement in relations between Mez and Kai, resulting in us having lunches together at school, like we'd always done prior to the incomprehensible animosity they had suddenly developed towards one another so recently. However, a couple of weeks into the new ceasefire which now seemed to exist between my two best friends, conversation inevitably turned to the exploits of *The Wardrobe*, especially as the first clear video footage of Kai-in-costume was plastered all over the internet.

Although the amateur footage had been captured using a mobile phone, it clearly showed Kai/The Wardrobe in crime-busting action, fighting off the attentions of four knife-wielding teenagers, easily disarming and incapacitating each of them before turning to stare down the owner of the camera-phone, the video stopping abruptly as its owner made their hasty retreat.

"Oh that's so staged!" Mez had sneered, tucking into her rabbit-food filled wrap as she watched the footage on her phone that lunchtime.

"What do you mean *staged*?" Kai had asked, trying to look as cool and uninterested as possible.

"Just look!" Mez said, thrusting the phone into his face, "Look at the way he stands there at the end, posing for the camera. You can almost smell the machismo seeping through the camera lens."

I could see Kai bristle, so attempted to diffuse the situation a little, taking a peek at the screen myself. "I genuinely think that whoever it is didn't know that he – if it is a *he* even– was being filmed."

Mez shook her head. "Of course they did. Out in the open, on a well-lit street…look at how the four *assailants* are equally distanced out around him."

"Perhaps they suddenly caught him unawares and surrounded him," Kai said calmly, "that would explain why he's in the centre of it all."

"Nah, that's been planned, rehearsed and perfectly

choreographed. No one is that quick at defeating four attackers…four guys all carrying knives, by the way. Either that or they got lucky."

"Lucky?" Kai snapped, causing Mez to smile wryly at him, "Do you think that its pure *luck* that someone is putting their life on the line, night after night, to rid this city of its evil?

Do you think it's pure *luck* that they have a 100% success rate so far? I'd say it more than damned luck!"

I shot Kai a glance, noting the way that Mez was keenly looking at him.

I'd seen her look at me like that when she tried to read me before and now I was pretty certain that she was trying to do the same to Kai.

Whether she found anything, I'm not altogether sure for the next thing I knew, Mez had shrugged her shoulders and taken another bite out of her wrap.

"Fair enough," Mez replied, "it's just a shame that he's not out there looking for Meggerlithick's real criminals rather than just making do with tackling the petty ones."

I glanced at Kai, raising my eyebrows, silently warning him not to take the bait.

But he did, swallowing it hook, line and sinker…

"What do you mean '*Meggerlithick's real criminalss*'? Those hoodlums in that video looked pretty damned serious from where I was sitting."

Mez screwed up the tin foil with the rest of her wrap in and expertly tossed in into a nearby bin.

"I accept that if the whole fight wasn't a set up then *The Wardrobe's* take down of those dudes looks pretty impressive, but they're small fry. He should

71

devote his attention to finding the real criminal masterminds out there, the powerbrokers not the pawns."

For a second, I could tell that Mez's statement had momentarily taken Kai aback before he calmly and quickly regained his composure.

"Like who?"

Mez smiled. "Oh, how would I know that? All I'm saying is let's see how well *The Wardrobe* would do were he to come up against a real supervillain, someone who'd use their brain instead of their brawn. Then we'd see how good they really were."

"Well, all I can say is that I'm glad that this is Meggerlithick and not Gotham City! One *super* on the streets is more than enough for me!" I laughed, trying to ease the tension which had suddenly reared its ugly head as Mez stood to leave the table, ready for our afternoon lessons.

"Me too," she smiled, adding, "Anyway, gotta run. Walk home with you tonight, AJ? We've got lots of catching up to do..."

# Chapter 8

As luck would have it, Kai had football training straight after school that night.

But I knew that it wasn't down to chance that Mez had suggested the two of us leave school together. She knew Kai was a creature of habit and would never, ever miss a training session, no matter how tempted he may have been to wonder why Mez would want to walk home with me that particular night, especially when she lived in totally the opposite direction, our school being exactly halfway between our two houses.

I suspected that Mez wanted to take me into her confidence about something and, sure enough, upon reaching Pinner's Newsagents, a matter of minutes away from my home, she suggested that we stop and grab an ice-cream.

"I've a favour to ask," Mez said as she dug into her Screwball with one of those useless plastic spoons that came with it.

Here it comes, I thought, biting down on the choc-ice she'd bought me, wondering what I would have to do to repay her for it.

Mez smiled, obviously seeing the anxious look on my face. "Hey, don't worry, I only want you to write a note to get me out of school tomorrow afternoon, just like the one you wrote last year."

To put the request into context, I'd probably best explain that my handwriting was almost exactly the same as Mez's mum's – I mean exactly the same. That's not to say that my handwriting is any good… Au contraire, mon ami!

No, it meant that Mrs Monroe' handwriting was the same spidery crawl as a teenage school pupil, a fact often remarked upon by Mez's PE teachers whenever they phoned to check that the notes excusing her from lessons due to her 'hypermobility' – a fancy way to say that Mez's joints were more flexible than others, often causing her issues in the past.

It was only when Mrs Monroe had let the headteacher have both barrels about constantly having to answer questioning phone calls, confirming whether she'd actually written the note whilst defending her poor handwriting that Mez could submit a note and not have it second-guessed by whichever teacher had taken possession of it that day.

However, upon realising that my own script now closely resembled her mum's, Mez had taken advantage of this happy coincidence on a few previous occasions, asking me to write notes claiming fake doctor, dentist and opticians' appointments, usually coinciding with a lesson where she failed to submit homework or a test that she hadn't bothered preparing for.

Mez always generously rewarded me for my efforts – the payment usually being some form of confectionery – and no one was ever the wiser about the deception (this included Mrs Monroe who the school now avoided calling to check the validity of the note for fear of incurring her wrath yet again).

"What do you need a note for Mez?" I asked, worrying that there was homework or an assessment due that I had forgotten about or not prepared for.

Mez looked at me over the top of her Screwball, a tiny glint of mischief dancing in her eyes. "I need to have the afternoon off tomorrow to sort out some stuff."

"What sort of stuff?"

She looked at me again, the pink plastic spoon now pursed between her lips. "It's probably best that you don't know."

"If I don't know why you want me to write you that note," I replied, "then I don't know if I'll be able to write it for you."

"Oh, when did you become so high and mighty? You wearing your special feisty pants today, AJ?" Mez sniffed, adding, "I was only trying to protect you, that's all,"

"I'd sooner you tell me," I replied, not altogether certain that I really wanted to know what my friend was planning to do.

Mez lifted the plastic cone which had contained her ice-cream and allowed the remains of it, the Screwball's multi-colours now merging as into one as they slid along together, to dribble into her mouth as she prised the bubble-gum ball that was stuck at the bottom out with the spoon, it's frozen outer-layer crunching as she bit down hard into it.

"Well if you must know," Mez finally said, her jaws enthusiastically chewing the gum, "I've a bit of business to attend to."

"What sort of business?"

"Like I said, the less you know the better it is for you," she replied, "let's just say that it's not just The Wardrobe – or whatever his stupid name is – who's helping to clean up this city – Mesmerise has been doing her bit too!"

Casually, she tossed the empty plastic cone at a

nearby bin, it hitting the rim before landing on the ground. Mez shrugged her shoulders as she turned to look at me.

I frowned, walked over to where the cone lay, picked it up and deposited it in the bin before I turned to look at her.

"When has Mesmerise been out on the streets, fighting crime? There's been nothing in the news at all about her, I mean, you at all!"

"Not all criminals skulk around in the shadows late at night, my young padawan," Mez replied, "some are a little more cunning, hiding behind the law, using things like politics and business backhanders to justify the pain and suffering that they cause to others. These are the real villains The Wardrobe should be going after, not just those on the street corners. Sometimes you have to dig a little deeper to find the dirty dealings that are secretly going on behind closed doors."

I went to reply, but Mez raised her hand as she always did to indicate that she hadn't finished talking, normally a quite endearing and eccentric gesture but one which irritated the hell out of me that day.

"I know you're just looking out for me," she smiled obviously seeing my face flush slightly, "but this is something that I have to do, you understand that, right."

"Sort of," I replied, still wondering just what Mez had been doing or planned to do next, "but I can't help thinking that you're not telling me the whole truth here."

"Aw, shucks, ya found me out copper!" Mez laughed in her appalling, fake, American accent, "And I would have got away with it if it wasn't for you damned, pesky kid!"

"Seriously, Mez," I replied, "what are you really up to?"

"Like I've already told you," she replied, jumping up from the bench that we'd both been sitting on, "I want to do my bit in putting all real bad guys away. I can't let The Wardrobe get all the damned glory now, whoever he may be!"

And so it was that the following day, having scrawled out my best 'please excuse Mez...' letter and watched as my friend skipped out of school that lunchtime, I sat with my parents in the living room eagerly awaiting the local evening news for a change.

My stomach was flipping somersaults as I waited for it to begin, recalling how Mez had waved at me as she'd casually strolled off, the helmet and ski-suit she'd previously purchased safety stowed away in the large holdall she'd brought to school with her that day.

Watching the titles roll accompanied by the dreary music that Go West had not sought to change since first transmitting their nightly news magazine way back in the last century, I couldn't help but wonder what my friend had gotten up to and whether it in any way matched – or bettered – the night-time escapes that my other super-friend was doing, secretly making an even greater name for himself.

In front of me, the cheesy-title sequence had finished and two presenters sat in a dimly lit studio, the camera slowly zooming in on them as the lights raised showing them both in their magnificent, white toothed glory.

"Good evening," the female presenter said, "and a warm welcome to tonight's edition of Go West. I'm Shabnan Nahar…"

"And, of course, I'm Sherman Dibnah!" Go West's ancient and legendary anchor-man smiled greasily, glowing as orange as ever.

"On tonight's programme…" his co-presenter continued.

Here we go, I thought nervously, let's see what the hell Mesmerise has been up to.

"Swine Fever," Sherman Dibnah boomed, "how a small Wiltshire village has got all hot and bothered over the ownership of an award-winning Gloucester Old Spot pig…"

I frowned, wondering how something so mundane would be keeping the sighting of another vigilante superhero from off the top of the show.

"Also coming up," Dibnah's co-presenter added, causing a flurry of excitement to build up in me again, "Gone to Pot…we meet Taunton's teenage snooker sensation hoping to sink a few big names at next month's World Snooker Championships. But first the news headlines read as always by Sherman…"

"Oh, this getting ridiculous!" I muttered, causing my dad cast a curious eye my way.

"Not like you to get so uptight about their cheesy-puns, AJ," he frowned, "everything all right?"

"Yeah, Dad," I replied, "I was just hoping that there might be something new about The Wardrobe on the show tonight that's all."

"Might be nice to hear something different for a

change," Mum replied, looking up from her knitting, "I don't know about you, but I'm a little bit tired with the press's obsessive coverage of him."

I was just about to reply when the smoothly hypnotic voice of Sherman Dibnah captured my attention from the television once again.

"Police are still questioning a man tonight after the disappearance of £100,000's worth of diamonds..."

There, on the screen was a shop that I instantly recognised, one that I'd passed dozens of times whenever I was in the city centre with either my family or friends.

"Isn't that..."

"Shhh!" Dad said, jabbing the volume control button on the remote control, "I'm trying to listen."

"The alleged theft," Sherman Dibnah continued as the screen filled with images of a very impressive looking shopfront, "took place in Smiths' Gold Jewellers in Meggerlithick sometime this afternoon."

Biting down on my lip, I leant forward desperate to hear every minute detail that Sherman Dibnah said as he continued to explain to the viewer the events which had taken place less than three miles from when I sat with my parents, glued to his news report.

"Unconfirmed reports suggest that the man who is currently in police custody is none other than the store's manager, Julian Greville-Ball, who catergorically denies all of the charges ..."

"Bit stupid to try and rob your own store, if you ask me," tutted my mum whose knitting needles hadn't stopped clicking throughout the broadcast.

"Hush, Magda," Dad scowled, I'm... trying... to... listen!"

"However, eye-witnesses claim that Greville-Ball was working with an unknown accomplice," Sherman Dibnah continued as the outside broadcast cut from looking at a photograph of the suspect to focus on two women stood, silently talking to one another in front of the store.

"Isn't that Lucy Laine from The Hungry Hippo?" Mum said, immediately recognising the landlady from the pub which Dad and Mum spent less time in than they would like given half the chance.

"Magda!" Dad grumbled as he pressed the volume control button yet again.

"…as I was about to pay," Lucy Laine was explaining to the unseen reporter, "I looked over and saw Mr Greville-Ball talking to someone."

"Did you see who it was?" the unseen reporter asked, shoving the microphone they held closer to their interviewee's face.

Lucy Laine shook her head. "I'm afraid not. They had their back to me, but I could tell by the way that Mr Greville-Ball was laughing and flirting that whoever he was talking to had made quite an impression on him…"

Don't ask me why but at that very moment, a cold chill decided to skateboard its way down the half-pipe that was once my spine as I waited for Lucy Laine to tell me what I somehow already knew and suspected.

"Like I said," she repeated, "I didn't catch a look at their face. But I did notice that they were wearing a ski-suit…"

*Strike one…*

"…it was black and gold…"

*Strike two…*

"…I remember thinking to myself that they looked like a bumblebee…"

*Strike three…my worst fears were out!*

"Can you please tell the viewer what happened next?" the unseen reporter pressed again.

"Well, it was most bizarre," Lucy Laine, who was obviously basking in the media attention that was being paid to her, added, "he reached under his counter, pulled out a tray and tipped its entire contents into the holdall that the other person held in their hands…"

Any lingering doubts I may have had were now totally dispelled as I immediately pictured Mez standing there, watching mischievously as the diamonds in the tray sparkled and glinted as they tumbled into the holdall she'd left school with less than seven hours earlier that day.

From the screen I vaguely heard the reporter ask Lucy whether she had seen the robber's face and I hoped with every ounce of my being that Mez had not been recognised.

Fortunately, Lucy Laine confirmed that she had turned away when Greville-Ball had looked directly at her, pretending to complete her own purchase.

"I turned to look at the other person as they left the shop," Lucy continued, "but by that time…"

*They already had a motorcycle helmet on*, I thought to myself, a fact soon confirmed by my parents' favourite landlady.

I got up to leave the room, my legs suddenly consisted of jelly as the reporter asked whether Greville-Ball had said or done anything once his accomplice had left the building.

Lucy Laine smiled. "No, he just stood there, gazing after whoever it was as though he'd been mesmerised by them…"

# Chapter 9

The following day, Mez wore the biggest grin imaginable as I approached the school gates, having obviously waited for me that morning rather than heading to the playground where we often would have met.

"So?" she smiled, almost bouncing up and down with excitement.

"So, what?"

Mez sighed. "You know full well what I'm taking about – *Go West* last night? Did you see what happened at Smiths' Gold yesterday?"

"Of course I did, it was pretty hard not to," I replied, "it dominated the whole of the news."

"And?"

"And what?"

I could tell that Mez's patience was beginning to wear thin, her face being the easiest of books to read when she was annoyed or upset.

Just like now.

"Why are you being so difficult, AJ?" she huffed, "If it's something that The Wardrobe has been up to, then you can't help raving on or gushing about it…"

"No, I don't."

"Do too," Mez ranted, continuing, "but as soon as Mesmerise appears on the scene, you pretend to act as though nothing she does even matters."

There it was again – Mez's insistence on referring to her super-alter-ego in the third person…

"That's probably because The Wardrobe is fighting crime," I snapped, "whereas Mesmerise…dammit, you, are using your powers to commit it instead!"

My outburst seemingly caught my friend totally unawares as she was momentarily speechless whilst I swept angrily past her, running to catch me up as I stormed towards class.

"Is that what you honestly think?" Mez asked, grabbing my forearm to stop me any further.

I swept it from her grasp and spun around to face her. "What else is there to think? Do you deny that you stole £100,000's worth of diamonds from the jewellers yesterday?"

"Yes," Mez replied calmly.

"See, you've admitted...huh? You're telling me that you didn't steal the diamonds, Mez?"

Now it was my turn to be completely blindsided by Mez's reply, or rather her firm denial.

Mez nodded. "That's right. I didn't steal the diamonds...Mr Greville-Ball simply donated them to Mesmerise's charitable causes!"

"Seriously?" I laughed, "Is that your way of justifying what you've done? You're no better than the criminals that The Wardrobe is putting behind bars, Mez. Not once has he done anything for himself, unlike what you did yesterday."

"AJ, you've got it all wrong," Mez sighed, gently holding my hand, "I'm not going to keep the diamonds. When the time is right, I will make sure that they end up in the hands of those that need them most, people far worse off than ourselves."

"Whose hands would they be then?" I frowned.

"All those the Greville family and their damned cronies have robbed blind and cheated," Mez replied, her face clouding, "Meggerlithick has been their own private plaything for years. So many families they've destroyed along with countless other lives ruined. As I've told you before, the worst kind of villains are the ones that hide in plain sight."

Just by looking at her I could tell that Mez genuinely believed that what she was doing was right and I began to understand her real motives, though I still didn't necessarily agree with her methods.

"Why doesn't Mesmerise just go to the media and tell them everything that she believes the Grevilles to have done?" I argued as the first morning bell rang, giving us a five-minute warning as to when school would begin.

Mez shook her head. "If only it were that easy, AJ. They run the city, nothing happens here with or without their say so. The mayor's a damned Greville himself for pity's sake! Who are they gonna believe, me or them? No, this way's better, at least until I have unearthed enough evidence I can use against I control the narrative and can start off by hitting them where it hurts them the most– in their pockets! In time, hopefully others will see what I'm doing and will come to understand and support my actions, you'll see."

"But Mez," I replied as we slowly made our way up the steps into school, "if you carry on stealing from them then it won't be long before the police will come after you. They'll see you as just a petty criminal, no better than the the ones that The Wardrobe is rounding up."

We'd reached the top of the steps as Mez stopped and smiled at me.

"Trust me, AJ," she winked, "by the time I'm through, the Grevilles won't just think of me as a criminal, they'll regard Mesmerise as their sworn nemesis, the ultimate supervillain!"

"And what about The Wardrobe? Wouldn't it be better if he knew your secret, that you're really on his side?"

Mez smiled. "Nah, let him try and work it out for himself. That way we'll see just how honest he really is. For all we know, he could be employed by the Grevilles to clean out some of the competition. The less that he, and anyone else for that matter, knows about Mesmerise, the better."

The second bell rang so we entered the building and scurried toward our respective classes.

However, there was just enough time for me to ask Mez one final question, the one that would cause me the biggest problem of my life were it to ever happen.

"Mez, what will you do if The Wardrobe catches you?"

"Trust me, that ain't ever gonna happen," Mez laughed, "but if it does, we'll just have to find out which one of us has the greatest superpowers I suppose!"

# Chapter 10

The next few weeks seemed to pass in a never-wordly blur as the press, local news, playground gossip and dinner-table chatter became more and more obsessed with the continued, and increasing, escapes of Meggerlithick's pair of celebrity-supers.

By night, The Wardrobe was cutting a swathe through the undesirable undergrowth – the poisonous weeds who had been choking our city, depositing those he'd overwhelmed and captured at the feet of a stunned and grateful police force.

But his achievements were continuing to be somewhat overshadowed by the charismatically daring exploits of Mesmerise, as now recognised by the press after Mez had deliberately left a handwritten receipt with her alter-ego's name scrawled all over it after *persuading* a security guard to cut out, roll up and hand her a rare and priceless Da Vinci sketch loaned to the city's museum by Lord Greville from his own personal and private collection.

Having carried out a series of raids, making off with an increasing haul of money, jewellery and other valuables, the press had taken to calling Mesmerise *'The Wardrobe's Arch Enemu'* even though the two of them had never come across one another when donning their customers to stalk the streets of the city. Had they have known that the two of them had actually known each other all of their lives but still had no idea as to what either of them was currently up to, they would have had an absolute field day.

No, it was once again left down to me to keep their secrets safe for them, and away from one another, which had suddenly become even more difficult again recently as there had been a total thawing of relations between Kai and Mez.

Thinking back on it, I suppose that whatever pent up anger and frustrations that they'd felt in their personal lives had suddenly been channelled elsewhere, Mesmerise and The Wardrobe allowing them the chance to *blow off steam*, for want of a better explanation.

Strange as it may seem but it some way I was glad as by living their secret lives the way they were meant that I got part of my life back – us three being back together as best friends again.

It started off slowly at first.

The odd meal here, going to the cinema there, but in no time at all we were back to how we were before Mez and Kai had developed their powers, spending more and more time together, both in and out of school.

There were even signs that the two of them were beginning to flirt a little with one another, a sure sign that whatever had driven a wedge between them had now been firmly removed, allowing the three of us to just enjoy being in each other's company once more. Of course, I had to remain vigilant and not reveal to either of them the secrets that both of them had sworn me to keep safe.

But it was a small price to pay to have a sense of normality return to my life.

Little did I know how fleeting it would be as the alternate universes that Mesmerise and The Wardrobe inhabited drew closer and closer on their inevitable collision course, ready to tear all our worlds apart…

It had all started innocently enough, film and pizza night at Kai's house, his parents being out as they often were, leaving him to his own devices yet again – a common occurrence which suited The Wardrobe's own nocturnal habits.

Having devoured three, large takeaway pizzas, we'd put the television on and were surfing the channels trying to come up with something that we could all agree on to watch.

"I fancy something a little bit sci-fi tonight, how about you?" Kai had said, his thumb repeatedly pressing the down key on his remote control.

"Nah, action and adventure all the way for me!" Mez had replied, flopping onto the couch whilst reaching for the coffee table, "Anyone want the last piece of garlic bread?"

Kai and I shook our heads.

"I don't know where you put it?" Kai laughed.

"Down here!" Mez replied, titling her head back as she slid the final piece of baguette in, almost swallowing it whole, like a gannet.

"Very ladylike," Kai frowned, his disgust compounded by the large belch Mez gave him by way of her reply.

"What about a comedy, Kai?" I asked, seeing no end to the stalemate that we had seemed to reach over our film preferences.

But Kai didn't seem to hear me, his eyes now fixed on the television screen, the local channel that he'd accidentally landed on seeming to be readying itself to show a live press conference, a fact confirmed by the scrolling text at the bottom of the screen.

"What is it, Kai? Mez asked having totally eaten the

garlic bread and slowly regained the power of speech. "I'm not sure, but it looks important," Kai replied as the camera zoomed in on an empty rostrum that now took centre stage.

As a portly looking middle-aged man made his way to the middle of the screen, his tight-fitting jacket struggling to contain his ample waist, Sherman Dibnah's dulcet tones filled the room as he began to commentate on the proceedings that were now unfolding before the three of us...

"If you're just joining us, dear viewer," Sherman Dibnah said sombrely, "the normal edition of Strictly Come Hiking has been interrupted to cover tonight's live briefing from the Mayor of Meggerlithick, Barrington Greville..."

"Sound ominous," Kai said, a frown masking his handsome features.

"Sounds dull and boring," Mez yawned, before taking another slurp of her coke.

"People of Meggerlithick," the mayor began, "I stand before you tonight a concerned citizen. Our city is in the grip of a crimewave unlike no other in its history. Honest, law abiding citizens are living in fear, waiting to be visited and robbed by the one who calls themselves Mesmerise..."

Now I would have thought it impossible to spit coke from the sofa onto the TV from where she was sitting, but that's precisely what Mez did, the liquid arcing from her mouth like a jet of water from a fountain before hitting the screen, narrowly missing Kai's ear.

"What the hell?" Kai shouted, quickly wiping the screen with the sleeve of his hoodie.

"Sorry, went down the wrong way," Mez lied as she

sat up and peered at the TV as the Mayor continued.

"...stealing their livelihoods and most treasured possessions. That's why tonight I am appealing to The Wardrobe, wherever he may be, to reach out to me. I promise that in return for the capture of Mesmerise, that all charges of vigilantism will be dropped against him..."

"The Wardrobe...a wanted man?" Kai gasped, turning to look at me, "But he's the good guy!"

"Depends which side of the fence you sit on by the looks of it, Kai," Mez replied, "don't you think, AJ?"

I didn't reply as I strained to hear the mayor end his speech.

"...failing that, a reward will be offered to any individual who helps lead to the capture and arrest of both Mesmerise and The Wardrobe. Goodnight."

Kai immediately turned the TV off and turned toward us, his face wearing the same expression as Mez's as they both stared at me.

It didn't take a genius to work out what they were both secretly thinking...would I rat out either one of them?

Quickly and subtly, I sought to allay their doubts.

"If I even suspected who either of them was," I chuckled, "I'd think twice about snitching them up! There'd be no telling what they'd likely do it they found out that someone had grassed on them, don't you agree?"

Knowing what I knew, it was almost hilarious seeing how relieved they then both appeared to be.

Still, I could tell by their faces that events had taken an unexpected turn and that both Mez and Kai were struggling to process the fact.

The three of us sat there silently for a moment as though the first person to break the tension which had built in the room would automatically lose the game. Inevitably, it was Mez who spoke up first.

"Well, that's definitely a game changer."

"How'd you mean?" I asked.

"Isn't it obvious? The mayor is being leaned on by all of his cronies as Mesmerise is relieving them of their ill-gotten games," she replied, letting her guard down slightly.

"You make Mesmerise sound like some modern-day Robin Hood," Kai replied, "whoever they are is no better that those that The Wardrobe is putting away. At least he's targeting those who prey on their victims at night, unlike Mesmerise."

I could see Mez bristle but most was impressed with how she managed to quickly retain her composure and not blow her cover as she responded.

"Funny how he's letting Mesmerise get away with things though, isn't it?"

*Don't bite, Kai,* I thought recognising Mez's preferred form of defence when backed into a corner – attack!

"*He's* letting them get away with it?" Kai repeated, his face reddening slightly, "Are you suggesting that Mesmerise and The Wardrobe are working together?"

"How else would you explain it?" Mez asked, clearly enjoying the fact that Kai had taken the bait, "Why else are they able to get away with the *crimes* they are committing without him swooping in and miraculously saving the day?"

"That's because Mesmerise is carrying them out during the daytime…"

*Big mistake,* I thought, wincing as I saw a small chink appear in Kai's normally impenetrable armour.

A chink that Mez quickly latched onto.

"You know what…that thought hadn't crossed my mind until now…"

You could almost hear the cogs spinning in Mez's head pondering this unexpected revelation.

Kai desperately looked at me for help as though I would be able to come up with a *one-size-fits-all* solution to the problem that he'd just inadvertently created.

"Perhaps he sleeps during the day," I replied, "after all, The Wardrobe must get incredibly tired from all that crime-fighting, not to mention the fact that he probably patrols the city streets throughout the night."

"Hmm, maybe..." Mez replied, not altogether believing my suggestion, but not totally disregarding it either, "or maybe he does another job during the day which means that he can't get out."

"Like what."

"Oh, I dunno. But – and I'm just spit balling here - but…" Mez was now revelling in the speculation, Mr Mischief having returned to sprinkle his impish fairy-dust into her naughty and playful eyes, "perhaps they work somewhere that they can't get out of easily, like a doctors' surgery, or a dentists…"

Kai and I looked at each other, somewhat relieved that Mez was no nearer to guessing his secret as Mez continued.

"But if he did work in one of those place then he'd be able to cancel or reschedule any of his appointments if he needed to. No, it would have to be somewhere where he couldn't get out of easily as he's constantly needed, like a…like a…"

"Like a what, *Sherlock*?" Kai smirked as a look of realisation suddenly dawned on Mez's face.

"Like…a school!"

Were it physically possible, I'm sure that I would have heard Kai's heart sinking deep within him judging by the look of horror that had suddenly filled his face.

I was also certain that had Mez had looked directly at him then at that very moment the game would have been up for him as The Wardrobe.

Fortunately, she didn't which allowed me the opportunity to reply instead, quickly deciding to try and throw her off the scent with a deliberate attempt at a double-bluff.

"Seriously? You think that a kid is The Wardrobe?" I laughed, looking at Kai, using my eyes to try and persuade him to join in, which luckily he did, though his forced laughter sounded slightly false and hollow.

"Nah, of course not," Mez replied, "can you imagine how difficult it would be for a kid to cut classes without someone suspecting something…"

*Oh, that's so damned clever,* I thought, *raising your suspicions of The Wardrobe whilst hiding the fact you've used more of the notes I've written you to go and commit your crimes as Mesmerise…genius!*

"No, not a kid," Mez continued, now in full conspiracy-theory mode, "an adult…a site agent, teaching assistant or…a teacher."

Kai looked at me and laughed, a mixture of relief and disbelief.

"Can you imagine Mr Pratt or Mr Blott as a superhero?" he grinned, "Blotty wouldn't say boo to a goose whilst Pratt-Features would struggle to catch a cold let alone a criminal!"

"Plus the fact he'd look like a lava lamp if he ever tried to run after someone," I added.

Mez frowned. "I'm not suggesting it's one of *our* teachers, I'm supposing that it might be *a* teacher. It would account for the fact that he never is about when Mesmerise is, wouldn't it?"

I knew that I would have to concede something to protect Kai but wondered about the dangers that might arise from this conversation ever existing.

"It's a good theory, Mez," I agreed, "but teachers normally have a strict moral code, don't they?"

"Whaddya mean?"

*What do I mean? Where am I going with this?* I remember thinking to myself when, out of absolutely nowhere, inspiration struck – and struck hard…

"Think about it…what do teachers always say to children who've been caught fighting, especially those that say '*it wasn't me, Miss, they started it?*'"

Mez thought for a moment, then shook her head. "Nope, you've got me there, what do they normally say, smarty-pants?"

"They always say '*Violence never solves anything*' or '*You shouldn't have taken the law into your own hands,*'" I replied, somewhat surprised with the ease in which I had put off the scent as to why The Wardrobe was never around during the day.

"I suppose you're right," she replied, "but you have to admit, it was a good theory, wasn't it?

"Yes it was, a damned good theory which makes me wonder something..." Kai replied, a little too enthusiastically for my liking.

Unfortunately, whilst throwing Mez off her particular line of enquiry, our whole conversation had now opened an entirely new one for Kai.

"And what might that be, Obi Wonder-Nobi?" Mez laughed.

"Maybe Mesmerise goes to school themselves," Kai replied, "that's why they aren't out on the streets at night – they're not allowed to be out late on a school night!"

Now it was Mez's turn to look slightly uneasy as Kai began to explain his reasoning as to why The Wardrobe – aka himself! – had never come across Mesmerise when patrolling the streets after dark.

"I bet that if you were to look at the times of crimes that they've committed," Kai continued, a newly-found excitement tinging his voice, "that they'll all have taken place somewhere between 9 am and 3.30 pm. Timings of a normal school day."

"But surely that would mean that they'd have exactly the same problem as someone who works in school, Kai?" I asked, now realising that Mez needed me to debunk his theory in much the same way as I had helped Kai do to lay her suspicions to rest just a few moments before.

"Yes, if they were *employed* by a school," said Kai, "but if they just *attended* school, then they would have far more opportunity to get out of lessons."

"In some schools, maybe," Mez suddenly blurted, "but our school is so hot on attendance that they check *every* absence or little request made, even checking that letters written and received are really from that person's parents. Ain't that right, AJ?"

*Ooh, you devious, little so-and-so*, I thought, knowing

exactly what Mez was playing at.

Agree and you provide her with a more solid form of an alibi if needed…

Disagree and leave yourself open to being landed in it with someone whose face was indicating that if she were to go down, then she would take me down too, kicking and screaming with her…

A rock and a hard place seemed to be a better option than being caught in between my two friends at that very moment, but I somehow sensed that no matter what I were to say that things would soon take a dramatic turn for the worse.

Nevertheless, I decided that, at this particular moment, discretion was probably the better part of valour…

"That's right, Mez. You know what it's like Kai, you've practically got to be dying to get let out of our school."

"In our year, maybe," Kai agreed, "but think about all of the other schools, sixth-forms and colleges in Meggerlithick. There has to be countless students who have study periods, free lessons and afternoons when they aren't supervised or don't need to attend every lesson in school. It would be so easy for someone to register as being in and then slip out to become Mesmerise."

A huge smile broke out on Mez's face as she began to relax, realising that she was as far away from unmasked as she ever would be.

"Well then, Kai," she replied, "you have to admit that Mesmerise, whoever they are, must have been touched by the hand of genius to have come up with such an airtight alibi as that."

"True. However, remember that they say that there is a fine line between madness and genius," Kai nodded, "and people like that often come unstuck when thinking that they are smarter than the rest. I'm sure that, given half-a-chance, The Wardrobe would prove to be more than a match mentally for Mesmerise."

I sat and watched quietly as Kai and Mez silently eyed each other.

For a moment, I wondered whether there was just the hint of recognition, that they'd sensed something in one another, but then as quickly as it may have appeared, it was gone and they were back to looking at each other the way normally did when the three of us were at our very best.

"You're probably right," I replied adding, "but, to be honest with you, if either one of them were that smart then we may never hear from either one of them again, at least for a little while."

"And why would that be, AJ?" Mez asked, Kai nodding in agreement at her question.

"You heard what the mayor said tonight," I answered, "that announcement not only declared war on Mesmerise, it also pinned a target on The Wardrobe's back. It doesn't matter their motives, good or bad, all the public will now see are pound signs whenever they appear, rightly or wrongly. I know that if either of them were me, I'd either retire immediately or, at the very least, lay-low for a few months to let the heat die-down and the dust settle."

Kai and Mez's eyes both dropped from mine, Kai finding the *OFF* button on the remote control whilst Mez picked at a piece of skin next to one of her fingernails, eventually biting it off before speaking

again.
"Think I'd do the same thing if I were in The Wardrobe's shoes, wouldn't you, Kai?"
Kai sat silently for a moment before slowly nodding. "I think either of them, if they had any sense, would hang up their masks for a little while at least…"

# Chapter 11

And do you know what?

Remarkable as it may seem, both of my friends – separately and secretly of course - decided that it would probably be prudent for them to take a break from their super activities.

Not that either one of them told me in so many words of course.

Part of it may have been due to the fact that they may have lost a little trust in me after the mayor's press conference.

After all, everyone has a price, as the saying goes.

Except for me.

I would never have given either one of them up, but I understood why they felt that they couldn't take the risk.

Let's face it, although the two of them had been blessed – or was that cursed? – with superhuman powers, they were still just a couple of teenagers who'd suddenly realised that what they were doing wasn't a game anymore and that there could be very real and dire consequences for them and those closest to them, myself included.

In truth, I was mightily relieved in more ways than one.

The first was obvious of course – I would no longer have to play *piggy-in-the-middle*, watching what I said and who I said it to.

Secondly, it was good to know that neither Mez nor Kai would be putting themselves in harm's way any longer whilst carrying out their own private and personal crusades.

But, finally, it meant that life could return to normal and we could all get back to what we were meant to be – teenagers, the stress of being one was quite enough for me, thank you very much!

So, for a while, we settled back into the old daily routine, the endless cycle of *school-home-homework-sleep-school* interrupted only by the salvation of spending time with my two best friends who were experiencing exactly the same trials and tribulations in their lives.

That was more than enough for me and soon, slowly but surely, it again became enough for Mez and Kai. Sure, there'd be the odd occasional glimpse of who they had both become, their frustrations at having to hide their alter-egos manifesting themselves occasionally.

But they managed to suppress these urges, each knowing deep-down that others close to them would be hurt the most were the truth ever to come out about their superhero identities.

Pretty soon, it was as though Mesmerise and The Wardrobe had never even existed.

The playground chatter died down, chats over the dinner table returned to how everyone's day had been at school/home/work* (delete where appropriate…) Newspaper headlines which had previously demanded an end to both of Meggerlithick's supers now desperately tried to fill their pages with articles asking where they had gone to, having seen their circulations plummet without the regular reports of Mesmerise and The Wardrobe to fill their column inches.

Even *Go West* had returned to reporting on dull, low-level local events in their news segments, anything from a cat with more than nine lives to the world's largest marrow dominating the top of the show which had previously dedicated itself to reporting the latest daily updates on Meggerlithick's daring duo…

Yes, life had quickly settled back into the same rut as before, which, for once, I was entirely grateful for, in the few, short weeks of peace we had before all hell broke loose again, bringing down the curtain on the story of Mesmerise and The Wardrobe…

It had all seemed so innocent enough at first – dinner with Mum and Dad, then our usual chat about the respective days that we'd had before I'd sat at the table with Mum, going through my homework whilst Dad watched *Go West.*

The nightly routine that we'd engaged in *before* Kai and Mez had become super…

The nightly routine that we'd had disrupted, watching the daily updates *whilst* Mez and Kai were Mesmerise and The Wardrobe…

The nightly routine that we'd returned to *after* Kai and Mez had, reluctantly, relinquished their alter egos and hidden their superpowers away again…

Even *Go West* was now firmly back in its boring and mundane routine, desperately trying, night after tedious night, to engage its viewer with something – anything – exciting about possibly the sleepiest and most uninteresting region in the country.

I'd not really paid that much attention to anything either Sherman Dibnah or Shabnan Nahar had twittered on about that evening, their inane *chitter-chatter* linking a succession of different TV spots ranging from the news headlines to sports and local events, punctuated with different 'special features' (and I, dear reader, use the term *special* in the loosest possible sense).

As usual, *Go West* was drawing to a close with the weather forecast following a recap of the news headlines- or should I say lack of them?

Then, just before the presenters took their leave for the night, Shabnan Nahar uttered the familiar words that would always precede the last segment of the show before the presenters would end with some cheesy pun, laughing as the lights faded and the credits rolled over an image of them tapping their papers onto their desks in the darkened studio...

"And finally, Sherman..."

Sherman Dibnah flashed his perfectly straight and white dentures at the camera.

"And finally, Shabnan, the city of Meggerlithick hasn't had a lot to cheer about recently..."

My ears pricked up and my eyes immediately turned to the screen as the image changed to show one of the city's oldest and most famous buildings as Sherman Dibnah's voiceover continued...

"The First Bank of Meggerlithick is the oldest private bank still operating in Great Britain, having been founded by Sir Granville Greville way back in 1672 and is still owned by his family, with his 10th, 11th and 12th generation descendants managing all of the bank's affairs, as well as their vast array of financial operations..."

My interest grew as Sherman Dibnah reeled off a range of bank services which the Grevilles offered to their 'high-net-worth clients' before explaining how they also almost exclusively provided the people of Meggerlithick with both business and personal loans, as well as mortgages, savings accounts, and tax and estate planning services.

"Oh, I do wish he'd get to the point," my mum tutted, "it sounds like a paid-for advertisement rather than a news report."

As though hearing her, Sherman Dibnah then revealed to the viewers the real reason why *Go West* was dedicating its final report to the Grevilles' private bank...

"...so to commemorate the anniversary tomorrow of its founding, the First Bank of Meggerlithick will be opening its doors early to customers, old and new, inviting them to visit a special and exclusive exhibition showing off some of the aspects of modern banking that they first introduced, such as printed checks, credit card readers..."

*Greville, more like Dullsville,* I thought to myself, suddenly finding my year 9 Maths homework far more interesting.

Undaunted, Sherman Dibnah refused to be ignored by me and continued to sell the exhibition as though he were a fairground worker desperate to entice people to his stand...

"However, the highlight of the exhibition promises to be the rare sighting of one of only nine £1,000,000 notes which ever circulated..."

"Can you imagine going into The Hungry Hippo and trying to pay for a round with that, Stefan?" my mum asked.

"Shush, Magda, I'm trying to listen!" came the expected reply, which I was grateful for as my ears pricked up once again…"

"…that's right, Shabnan," Sherman Dibnah was now saying to his co-presenter back in the studio, "it is incredibly rare and valuable, being one of only two ever recovered after all nine ever printed were stolen back in 1990."

"Will you be going to see it?" Shabnan Nahar asked as *Go West's* theme tune began to quietly play in the background.

"Absolutely," Sherman Dibnan smiled, "but, like you dear viewer, I'll have to make sure that I am there bright and early as the doors open at 9 am."

"Make sure that you dress to impress them then, Sherman," Shabnan Nahar giggled, "you need to look in *mint* condition so that they let you in."

Sherman Dibnah laughed loudly and falsely. "Oh, don't you worry, Shabnan, I'll make sure that I look a million bucks as I am sure that there will be lots of interest in being so close to something that rare."

Just then, something dragged a long, cold finger down the length of my spine as an image suddenly popped into my head – an image of someone who may have more than a passing interest in being up close and personal to something so rare, so valuable and so precious to the Greville family…

*Please, let me be wrong,* I thought to myself as I watched the two self-satisfied presenters laughing with one another on screen as it faded to black, as black as my dreams proved to be that night…

# Chapter 12

The dark circles which ringed my eyes the following morning as I looked in my bathroom mirror only reinforced my first suspicions – my sleep had been as fitful and disrupted as I'd suspected it had been.

On waking up and looking at the duvet cover, which had seemingly been hurled across my room, and my pillows laying on the floor beside my bed, initially confirmed the fact that it must have been one helluva nightmare I'd experienced, my bedroom the night-time battleground in which my dreams were violently fought.

However, it wasn't the state of my room that concerned me the most – it was the fact that I could only recall a snippet or two of the dream that had obviously caused me such distress as to thrash around, hurling bedclothes asunder.

Normally, when you initially open your eyes first thing in the morning, there are some fragments of your nightmare that still cling to you, their claws embedded deep in your first waking moments, refusing to let you go, causing you to initially doubt what is real or not.

Slowly, but surely, you recognise that they are just figments of either an over-active or an overtired imagination and you begin to think whether, sub-consciously, your dreams are actually trying to tell you something.

Normally, that happens…

But not this day.

This day, no matter how hard I tried, I just couldn't

retrieve what my dreams had been about and whether they had been good or bad.

Probably bad, I suspected.

My mind was fuzzy…hazy, like I was supposed to remember something…do something…say something.

Briefly, out of the shadows of my mind, three figures began to appear.

Slowly, as they became clearer, it was patently obvious that two of the figures were Mez and Kai… Naturally!

However, what threw me was the fact that the third person, the third figure I could see, as clearly as I see this computer, which I am writing this recount to you on, was none other than yours truly….

The one, the only…AJ Sipowicz, no less, albeit a slightly bluish version of myself, as though I had been badly photoshopped there.

Now, I know what you're thinking to yourself - '*it's bad luck to see yourself in a dream*' or '*it's impossible to see yourself in a dream*' but in fact, neither claim is actually true, both just the result of what my mum would call '*old wives' tales*'.

However, it was the first time that I'd ever dreamt of myself in the third person and do you know the first thing I thought to myself…?

'*You need to knock a few of those late-night visits to the fridge on the head, my dear Sipowicz!*'

After that initial thought, I then wondered what I was saying to both Mez and Kai, who were stood furiously looking at me.

Try as I might though, I could not make out a single word, no matter how hard I strained my ears or rewound the scene in my head trying to lipread what I was saying to my friends, the skills I'd learned when passing every hearing test until the age of six with glue-ear failing me miserably.

I tried to make out where or when I was, trying to work out the surroundings we were stood in, but these soon faded away, leaving me and my friends in my *Sleep Studios* silent movie production.

Slowly, the three of us began to disappear, leaving me no nearer knowing what my subconscious mind was trying to tell me, if anything at all.

I looked at my clock:

7:30 am.

*Plenty of time to get ready – oh sh…*I thought to myself, suddenly remembering something important which may have triggered the dream…

The First Bank of Meggerlithick's exhibition today.

"That must be it!" I whispered, quickly scrambling for my mobile phone, hoping against hope that there'd be no message from Mez telling me that she wouldn't be in school today, effectively falling off *supers'* wagon, back into the arms of Mesmerise.

I held my breath, turning the phone from its facedown position, the screen automatically coming straight back to life.

Breathing the hugest sigh of relief, I put the phone back down again, relieved that the text that I dreaded the most that morning had failed to materialise.

All was good with the world – Mez obviously hadn't seen *Go West* and so was blissfully unaware of the million-pound banknote that the Grevilles no doubt valued more than anything else in their over-indulged world.

"It's gonna be a good day after all," I said to myself as I jumped into the shower…

Without giving a second thought to my nightmare or its potential hidden meaning, I was soon on my way again, running the hamster-wheel of my school life, its seemingly never-ending educational cycle beginning yet again.

I swear that as I was getting older, the length of the time I spent in school seemed to be growing, terms lasting years instead of weeks.

Finally, I arrived at the school gates, my mind having wondered through a myriad of random teenage thoughts, none of them any different to those that any ordinary fourteen-year-old would randomly be thinking.

There, waiting for me was Mez, the infectious smile that melted the hearts of all that she came across painted broadly across her face.

"Hey, AJ, all good?"

I smiled.

*You're here at school and not at the bank, so yeah, actually I am,* I thought, nodding and smiling back at her.

"Wicked!" Mez replied as the two of us began to walk through the gates, "Actually I'm glad to be back in school this morning for a change. Mum took me to meet her new fella straight from school last night. Man, does he love himself…"

I listened to her ramble on with an inane grin on my face, finally reassured that she had been nowhere near a television screen last night and so hadn't seen last night *Go West.*

Eventually, we occupied our usual positions on the low-built wall that ran alongside the steps into our school block.

Mez continued to fill me in on the events that had occurred the previous evening, leaving out no detail, no matter how gory they first appeared…

"…but as we talked over dinner, I couldn't help but look at his beard and notice how there were several little specs of food which seemed to have got caught up in it, like those flies that get trapped in your nan's net curtains during the summer, you know what I mean?

Laughing, I nodded that I did, and if I couldn't quite visualise it myself, Mez's words were continuing to paint an unpleasant and unwanted picture in my mind…

"It wasn't so bad when we had the main course," she sighed, "but when we got to pudding, it was rhubarb crumble and custard and then he got some of it on the bottom of his moustache, which looked like…hang on a sec, someone's buzzing me."

Mez reached into the back of her school trousers and pulled out her phone, running a finger up its screen to unlock it whilst I watched the world go by.

"Hmmm," Mez mumbled, her lips pursed as a cloud of a frown began to form on her brow.

"Everything all right?"

"What? Yep…fine," she replied, the beginnings of a smile reappearing, disarming me, causing me to drop my guard a little, "It's just Mum. Can I borrow your phone to reply, I'm forget to top up the credit on mine."

"Sure thing," I replied, retrieving it from my backpack and handing her it without looking, "my passcode is-"

"Your birthday backwards," Mez replied absent-mindedly, tapping in the six-digits, before scrolling through the screens, pausing momentarily before tapping away on the screen, biting her bottom lip as she did so.

By now, the playground was filling up ready for the first bell, which duly rang.

I stood to join the line and felt a tug on my backpack as Mez dropped my phone back into it.

"Thanks," Mez smiled, as she stood alongside me, "Mum would have had the search parties out if I hadn't have answered her straight away!"

"Might be a good thing that she's got a new boyfriend to keep her occupied then," I laughed as more and more children joined the line that we'd inadvertently started.

"You could be right," Mez laughed, "even with his custard-covered whiskers!"

After the second bell had rung, we walked together a little way, laughing about Geoff – that was the new boyfriend's name – and his poor eating habits, stopping only to say goodbye to one another before heading off to our separate form rooms.

"See you at lunch?" Mez asked, that huge smile now firmly fixed back on her lips.

"Unless hell freezes over!" I replied, awaiting her usual response of *'Good job I'm hot stuff then!'*

But Mez had already turned and sped off, leaving me to think that she was in more than a hurry to get to her form than usual.

Pondering this, I turned, put my backpack in my

locker and then walked into my form room, ready to greet Kai when he eventually arrived.

For someone as honest and straight as him, I put his general tardiness in arriving at school on time down to one or two things.

Of course, when he was The Wardrobe, his late night activities had been a good enough excuse for me, but he'd always been a late arrival way before those days. No, Kai simply either didn't see the point in rushing to get anywhere or had always been afflicted with the teenage curse of *lazyitis* even before he turned thirteen,

Still, I thought nothing unusual about his lateness as I sat at my desk, watching the classroom fill up, Miss Lee her usual cheery self at the front of the class...

However, after she had taken registration and Kai's seat was still unoccupied, a horrible dread began to wash over me as he was never absent, something of cataclysmic proportions would had to have happened to prevent him from attending school.

And even on the incredibly rare occasions when he was off school, he would always call or text me to tell me why...

It was then that my stomach fell through the floorboards, an overwhelming, impending sense of doom filling every fibre of my body.

Instinctively, I raised my hand.

"Yes, AJ?" Miss Lee replied.

"Miss, may I go to the toilet please?"

Miss Lee gave me the look – you know, the one that says *'Shouldn't you have gone before registration?'* – but must have realised by the pained look on my face

that I really had to leave the room immediately.
"Very well, but don't go making a habit of it."
I rushed out of my seat, my sudden urge to leave the class only reinforcing that my need to be excused was as desperate as I'd first implied.

Outside, I went straight to my locker and fumbled around inside my backpack, my hand eventually settling on the phone, which, unsurprisingly, nestled right at the bottom beneath everything else jumbled up in there.

I closed the locker door, sneaked a quick look around to check that I hadn't been observed, then darted to the toilets, selecting the cubicle furthest away from the door, as the hero always does in the movies.

Flipping the toilet seat down, I sat on it and tapped in my passcode, before selecting the *Messages* icon.

My heart sank as I saw that Kai's name was now at the top of the list of names of messages received.

It plunged deeper when I noted that his texts did not have the little blue dot to the left of them indicating that they had yet to be read.

"Mez," I sighed as I clicked on Kai's name to read what he had sent me.

As per usual with Kai, he had sent multiple messages, rather than typing all of his thoughts into one single text...

**KAI: Hi, sorry, but I'm not going to be in today.**

Kai always insisted on typing his texts so that they were grammatically correct too, the only concession he'd occasionally make would be to include the odd emoji every now and then...

**KAI: Can you tell Miss
Lee that I'm sick.**

What was it with my friends that they'd always
assume that I would do their dirty work when they
wanted to skive off?
However, like I've said, Kai never used to skip
school, so I knew that he had ulterior motives...

**KAI: I'm not really, just
fancied bunking off**

So far, so boring, I could feel my fluttering heart
begin to settle a little at seeing that Kai's messages
were so mundane that nobody would suspect
anything, not that it appeared to be anything other
than an extreme bout of *lazyitis* that he was clearly
suffering from.
However, as I continued to read, I felt my body
suddenly turn cold as the true reason behind his
unexpected absence became all too painfully clear...

**KAI: In fact, I'm feeling like
a million dollars!** 😌

"No, no, no, no, no..." I cried, unable to tear my eyes
from the screen...

**KAI: So I will probably
check out the Grevilles'
special exhibition at the
First Bank!**

*This can't be happening,* I thought, my head beginning to swim a bit, my worst fears confirmed by Kai's final, cryptic message...

KAI: I hope I don't bump into
anyone I know! 😊

I felt sick to my stomach, understanding exactly what Kai, or rather The Wardrobe, was planning to do that morning.
He must have believed when watching *Go West* the night before that Mesmerise may have also seen the report and would view it as an ideal opportunity for one, final act of revenge against the Grevilles.
But Mez hadn't watched *Go West* and so would have had no idea about the million-pound note until she read Kai's texts.
However, as I stood there, trying to catch my breath, I still couldn't quite believe that Mez had deliberately misled me and had actually looked at my phone.
After all, she'd only borrowed it to answer her mum's message, hadn't she?
Looking at the last two messages on Kai's message timeline then confirmed my worst fears and sent my world spiralling out of control.
The first he had sent twenty minutes after his previous one, an unusually long one from him for a change...

KAI: Hi AJ, hope all is OK.
As I haven't heard from you,
I've text Mez and asked her
to get you to check your phone.

Don't want school phoning my
parents now! Let me know you've
read them please. x

This text was followed by the reply that had been sent
on my behalf...

ME: KK, Must b somethin pretty
spesh 4 u 2 skip skool.Dontcha
worry I'll cover 4 u x Have fun!

*God, she knows me so well,* I remember thinking as
the toilets began to whirlpool around me, faintly
marvelling at how my friend could perfectly replicate
the way that I answered my texts.
As the tiled floor began to loom large as I fell towards
it my final thoughts were that the game was finally up
for all of us as my world suddenly descended into
darkness...

# Chapter 13

Slowly, out of the darkness, I saw a blurry image begin to appear which I soon recognised as that of the old 17<sup>th</sup> century building that had dominated the centre of Meggerlithick for close to four hundred years.

The sky above it was bright and the buildings around it much younger and totally out of character with its classical architecture.

Beside it ran an alley where the old and the new buildings of the city met, an alley my friends and I had walked down on many occasions in the past.

Only now I saw Mez striding past the line of people who were queued down the alley waiting to enter the First Bank of Meggerlithick.

Heads would turn towards her, ready to protest at her jumping the queue, only to be silenced with one turn of Mez's head, smiles and peaceful looks now replacing the frowns that they'd worn before being mesmerised and seduced by her charms.

As Mez rounded the corner and moved to the front of the line before making her way up the huge, impressive steps to the building, out of the corner of my omnipresent eye I thought that it saw movement behind some huge industrial rubbish bins in another alley on the other side of the busy High Street.

However, I paid no more that a passing interest to it as my mind's eye quickly refocussed on Mez as she smiled and easily passed the security guards at the entrance to the bank, winking at them through the part her helmet where the visor would normally be, her eyes still the only exposed part of her face once again.

Suddenly, there was a swirl of black as the bins rattled and the tall, imposing figure of The Wardrobe dashed through the oncoming traffic and raced up the stairs into the bank, Kai not quite travelling at the speeds that I knew him capable of.

Again, the security guards paid no heed to his arrival, nodding once at him as he flew up the steps and into the building, Mesmerise having already begun to make her way up to the first floor.

Suddenly, the air was filled by the wailing of sirens as large, red lights began to flash at various points on the bank as thick, steel bars dropped down into every doorway and window, instantly transforming the look of the building into that of a high security prison.

More sirens wailed as police cars and vans mounted the pavement, a large number of heavily armed officers wearing protective clothing made a cordon around the building, moving onlookers away to a safe distance.

My view shifted from window to window, desperate to see what was happening inside but, at first, I could see no further than the barricades which had been put in place.

Then at one of the windows on the third floor, I suddenly saw Mez's face.

She had removed her helmet and had pressed her face against the glass, her lips moving frantically, desperately trying to make herself heard to me…

"AJ…AJ…Can you hear me?"
The first face I saw when I opened my eyes was Mrs Dhanda, the school nurse who was smiling back down at me.

"You gave us quite a scare there."

"Where am I?" I asked, making to sit up only for Mrs Dhanda to gently place a hand on my shoulder.

"Not so fast, you took quite a tumble in the toilets. Luckily, Miss Lee sent Ashley to check on you so it wasn't too long before we found you. How are you feeling?"

"All right, apart for the banging headache," I said, raising my hand to my forehead, feeling the egg that had started to grow there, "feel a bit sick, mind." That part wasn't strictly to do with my fall, it was more likely caused by my recollection of the vision I'd had whilst I lay unconscious.

However, I needed Mrs Dhanda to think that I definitely had concussion to help get me out of school.

She nodded knowingly. "Think that it probably best to give either your mum or dad a call to get you home. Who would it be best to call?"

"What day is it?" I asked, deliberately playing up my symptoms.

"Thursday," Mrs Dhanda frowned.

"Mum then, she doesn't work Thursdays."

Mrs Dhanda nodded. "I'll just go and phone home from the office then. Mrs Simmons will sit with you until I get back. However, if your mum can't get here straight away, is there a friend that you would like to sit with you until she does?"

"Mez Monroe," I replied no sooner than she had finished speaking, quickly adding, "please."

Mrs Dhanda nodded at our school secretary as she went to the office to phone home.

I lay back on the nurse's couch and closed my eyes,

partially because of the splitting headache that was now in full effect, but also praying that Mrs Dhanda would return with Mez, proving all of my premonitions and suspicions to be wrong.

Unfortunately, when Mrs Dhanda returned alone five minutes later, my worse fears were quickly realised.

"Mum says that she's on her way to your nan's at the moment but will turn around and should be here within half and hour," Mrs Dhanda said, adding, "Unfortunately, Mez has just left school as she has a hospital appointment and is not expected back. Is there anyone else in school that you'd like to sit with you?"

"No thanks," I replied, a vice-like grip tightening around my stomach, "I'll be all right to wait with you, Mrs Dhanda, until my mum gets here..."

Fortunately, as I knew she would, Mum was at school in half the time she'd suggested, no doubt doing her best Lewis Hamilton impression when driving across Meggerlithick.

Within another ten minutes, I was sat in front of the car, Mum bombarding me with questions, asking whether I'd like to go to A&E to get checked out.

"I'm fine, Mum, honestly," I replied, flicking the radio on trying to catch the 10 am local news, "if we go there, we'll probably spend the next three or four hours waiting only for them to confirm what Mrs Dhanda already suspects. Please can we just go home instead?"

My mum looked at me and nodded. "Only if you promise that if you start to feel any worse then you'll tell me straight away."

"I will Mum, promise."

Luckily for me, my mum wasn't the sort of person to make a drama out of a crisis and also knew how sensible I was when it came to things like my health. Normally.

Today though, my reluctance to go to hospital was based on two things.

Firstly, having wasted most of the day waiting to be seen, the hospital would then *probably* tell us that I *probably* had minor concussion and that my parents would have to keep a close eye on me for the next forty-eight hours.

This would be nothing new for Mum and Dad as they'd had to monitor me for a couple of days once before when I fell off the swing at the local park and smacked the back of my head on the tarmac, a small crescent scar now a permanent reminder of my seventh birthday.

Secondly, I wanted to get home as soon as possible to try to contact either of my super-friends to warn them of my premonition and the possible trap that may be awaiting them at the bank.

But before that, I needed to make sure that I wasn't already too late, hence my enthusiasm in searching for the local news on Mum's car radio.

Fortunately, by the time her car had swung onto our driveway, not a word had been uttered, nor a newsflash made regarding the capture of either Mesmerise or The Wardrobe.

I felt some of my nausea subside as we walked through the front door and I began to walk up the stairs to my room.

"And where do you think you're going?" my mum

asked, giving me *that* look that all parents seem to automatically inherit once they have children of their own.

"Up to listen to some music," I lied.

"I think it best you stay down here where I can keep an eye on you."

"Mum, I'm fine, honestly," I replied, "apart from the unicorn horn growing out of my head, I feel tip-top!"

Mum frowned at me, you know, the mind-reading frown where they try to work out whether you are lying or not.

Fortunately, her spidey-senses didn't notice anything unusual in my reply as she slowly nodded her head.

"OK, but I will be checking on you," she smiled, "and, if you start to feel sick or sleepy, call me. Promise?"

"Promise, Mum," I replied, wearing my falsest, cheesiest smile, before turning and sprinting for my room.

No sooner had I closed my bedroom door than I had retrieved my phone, tossing my backpack against my wardrobe, flopping down onto my bed, propping myself on my elbows, frantically texting with both my thumbs.

I thought about sending a message to them both at exactly the same time, but part of me still clung to the hope that they still didn't know about each other, so I text them separately.

First Kai…

ME: Kai txt me, URGENT!
Danger – dontcha go 2 the
bank – it's a trap x

Then Mez...

ME: Mez pls txt, URGENT!
Don't go 2 the bank
– it's a trap x

I lay there, staring at the screen, willing it to vibrate,
not once, but twice, my friends telling me to '*chillax*'
and that all was good with them and that I was
'*worrying about nothing*', causing me to feel foolish
at making such a big fuss as neither of them had
returned to their super ways...
Only my texts remained unanswered.
In fact, neither text showed as being delivered,
meaning that either both of them had turned of their
phones or they were somewhere where they were
unable to receive my texts...
"Oh no," I gasped, a new wave of nausea flooding my
senses as I sat bolt upright on the side of my bed.
I went to stand, but my legs gave way underneath me
as the room begin to spin like the inside of a washing
machine on its final cycle, as darkness once more
took my hand and led me away...

# Chapter 14

.... toward the old 17<sup>th</sup> century building which had
dominated the centre of Meggerlithick for centuries
The sky was still bright, the sun still dazzling,
bouncing off the windowpanes of the younger
buildings which stood surrounding the bank.

I looked up the alley which separated the old and the
new parts of the city to once again see Mesmerise
striding past the queue that had formed to gain entry
to the exhibition being held in the First Bank of
Meggerlithick.

As before, heads turned towards her, protesting as she
skipped the queue, their protests silenced by her
smiling eyes as she looked at each and every one of
them, contentment spreading through the line as my
friend passed them, a noticeable bounce in each and
every step that she took.

However, this time as Mez rounded the corner,
heading towards the front of the line and the huge,
stone steps leading up to the building, my focus
deliberately shifted to the movement I had seen
behind the industrial rubbish bins in the alley beside
the department store on the opposite side of the High
Street.

This time I could clearly see The Wardrobe's face as
he looked over the bins, watching Mesmerise's arrival
at the bank, ready to spring from the shadows to
capture her his eyes keenly watching her every move,
as did mine as I returned my gaze toward her as she
approached the two security guards standing on either
side of the forbidding entrance.

But before she could advance any further, Mesmerise was stopped in her tracks as a little girl, dressed all in blue, came running out of the bank, clutching a bright red balloon in her hand.

"Look what the nice man gave me," I heard her say to Mez, swinging the hand holding the ribbon tied to the balloon.

But before Mez was able to comment, the little girl lost hold of the ribbon and the balloon swept away from her.

"My balloon!" the little girl cried, running down the steps to chase after it as it floated across the pavement.

"No…don't!" I heard Mesmerise scream as the little girl chased the balloon, oblivious to everything except the balloon as it drifted away from her towards the onrushing traffic.

She began to chase after the girl, taking two steps at a time as she desperately tried to close the gap on her. Behind her, one of the guards raised a walkie-talkie to his lips and shouted 'suspect sighted, send backup now' but Mesmerise was oblivious, her mind solely focussed on saving the little girl from going under the wheels of an oncoming vehicle.

Across the street, I now saw that The Wardrobe had realised what was happening and was now rushing towards the traffic himself, hoping that his superhuman speed and strength would help him reach the little girl before it was too late.

Unfortunately, it was.

"Got it!" the little girl laughed, jumping up and clutching the ribbon, standing in the middle of road having miraculously avoided any traffic in doing so.

"Look!" she smiled, turning to face Mesmerise who was nearly upon her, The Wardrobe having left the kerb on his side of the road at the same exact moment.

Both Mesmerise and The Wardrobe's arms wrapped around the little girl a couple of seconds before the double decker bus hit the three of them.

"Look!" the little girl said again as she grew, her whole body turning blue, the red balloon now transforming into a full head of hair as *I* transported my friends out of the street and onto the top of the First Bank of Meggerlithick...

"What the hell just happened?" I said as I sat on the edge of my bed in my room at exactly the same moment as the *other* me said the same thing as the three of us reappeared on the roof of the building.

"You're asking us?" The Wardrobe asked, taking an unsteady step back, looking at both Mesmerise and myself in confusion, "I mean, why were you were a cute, little girl one minute and the next you're... you're...this *thing*?"

"Never mind that," Mesmerise said excitedly, "That was so awesome! Damn! You sly dog! So, what superhero name do you use?"

"I...I..." I stuttered - or should I say - *we* stuttered, "I don't have one, this has just suddenly happened to me today."

"Well, judging by the red hair and blue body, you could always call yourself something mysterious like..." Mesmerise paused for a minute, "like *Le Grand Schtroumpf!*"

Both of me – the one in the room and the one on the roof – struggled to work out the English translation, French being a subject *I/we* never particularly paid much interest in, or attention to, at school.

Kai shook his head and sighed. "It translates to *Papa Smurf*, AJ!"

"Wait – how do you know that?" Mesmerise asked turning sharply to The Wardrobe.

"Why, aren't superheroes supposed to know how to speak French?" The Wardrobe snapped, "Or is that the exclusive right of a supervillain like you?"

*Oh God, I/we* thought as Mesmerise and The Wardrobe squared up to one another, *here it comes...*

"Not French, dummy," Mesmerise replied, "that their real name is AJ?"

For a moment, *I/we* could see a moment of doubt flicker across The Wardrobe's eyes, either indicating that he'd realised that he'd made a terrible error by calling *me/us* by *my/our* real name or was it a sudden recognition as to who it really was hidden behind the motorcycle helmet?

It proved to be the latter...

"Because AJ's one of my best friends," Kai said, taking off his mask, "along with you, Mez."

Mesmerise's head snapped from Kai to *me/us* back to Kai before she began to laugh loudly, taking her helmet off in the process.

"Man, now that is what I call a cool plot twist!"

"Tell me about it!" Kai chuckled before a more serious look clouded his face as he looked at *me/us*, "How long have you known about Mez, AJ?"

"I...I..." *I/we* stuttered, grasping for an answer which *I/we* just couldn't find.

"Right from the very start," Mez replied, adding, "as was probably the case with you, right, Kai?"

Kai nodded then sighed. "I don't know whether to be angry with you or whether to apologise, AJ."

"Why would you want to apologise to me?" *I/we* replied.

"Because we both made you swear to keep what you knew a secret no doubt," Mez replied, placing her hand on *my/our* arm, "you're a good friend AJ."

"Thanks, " *I/we* replied, "but I don't feel like one."

"Why not?" Kai replied, "You've just saved both of our lives. How did you know we would both be here at this exact moment? I never told you what time I'd be here..."

"And I never said anything to you about skipping school after finding out about the exhibition," Mez replied.

Mez and Kai stood transfixed as *I/we* told them about *my/our* dreams and premonitions.

*I/we* showed them the bump on *my/our* head and how at that very moment in time there were two of *me/us* talking to them in unison – one at home sat on the bed, whilst the other one stood talking to them after the rescue.

The *bedroom-me* and the *blue-me.*

Mez and Kai looked at one another and shook their heads.

"So, let me get this straight, there's now two of you?" Kai asked.

*I/we* shook our heads. "I don't think so. It's really hard to explain."

"Try us," Mez replied.

"It's like I'm in two places but at exactly the same

time as I have the same thoughts and say the same things, but my actions and movements are totally separate and different. You understand?"

Kai looked at me sceptically. "I'm not quite sure I do, I mean, why would you suddenly split into two versions of yourself?

"Because of the fall," Mez replied, "your mind was obviously starting to alter, hence your nightmare, but the bang seems to have sped up your transformation into something more, something else, something... *super*."

*I/we* looked at Kai but could tell that he wasn't convinced by my explanation. *I/we* decided that there was only one way that *I/we* could convince him otherwise.

"I think Mez is mostly right," *I/we* replied, "but when I got no reply to the texts I sent you both before this happened, then the adrenaline from the fear that I felt must have completed the transformation."

Mez and Kai both reached for their phones, seeing the texts that they'd failed to respond to.

It was then that *I/we* saw the perfect opportunity to prove that *I/we* could really be in two places at once.

"Text me," *I/we* said, the *bedroom-me* picking up the phone, whilst the *blue-me* held their empty hands out in front of them, "ask me something only the version of me standing in front of you could possibly see."

Kai looked at his phone suspiciously, but Mez was already texting away frantically on her phone, hitting the *SEND* button, causing the phone to buzz in the hand of *bedroom-me*.

*I/we* waited until Kai finally sent his text before replying, my friends' phones buzzing at exactly the same moment.

"I don't believe it!" Kai said shaking his head as Mez laughed hysterically as she read the text that *I'd/we'd* copied them both in…

**AJ: My 2 BFFs, standin beside each other opposite a red-haired smurf on the roof of the bank wondering how the hell we get ourselves out of this mess…**

"OK," Kai replied, "I believe that you actually are in two separate places at once, even though I'm not quite sure *how* you can be."

"Neither am I, Kai," *I/we* said, "the only way I can describe it is that I feel like I'm…like I'm…"

"Multi-tasking!" Mez laughed, clapping her hands in delight, "You're The Multitasker!"

*I/we* laughed. "That's as good a superhero name as any name, I suppose!"

Mez and *I/we* laughed hysterically as Kai shook his head, a wry grin beginning to form on his lips. However our laughter was interrupted by the sound of sirens as Kai slowly walked to the edge of the building and looked over the edge down at the pavement below.

Mez and *I/we* joined him, watching as dozens of police officers jumped out of the vehicles below and began to search the streets around the bank.

"Looks like the three of us are now wanted fugitives," Mez frowned as people flooded out from the bank, ushered out by the security guards, closing the doors behind them when the last of the bank employees had left the premises.

"We might probably be in the safest place in Meggerlithick for the moment," Mez said, "they won't think to look at us on top of the bank now, will they!"

"No," Kai replied, "but it'll only be a matter of time before they come back and search the building."

The *blue-me* extended their hands towards *my/our* friends. "Come on, let me see if I could transport us away from here."

Kai went to take a hand but Mez stood her ground and shook her head.

"I'm not going until I finished what I started, especially as I now have the perfect opportunity to do so whilst the bank is empty and unalarmed."

"I was going to overlook what you've been doing after our near miss and because of our friendship," Kai said grimly, "but if you attempt to steal anything else, I will stop you."

"I'd like to see you try!" Mez replied, trying to stare Kai down, despite the vast difference in height between them.

"Don't make me do it, Mez."

"Then don't try and stop me, Kai!"

*I/we* sighed and shook *my/our* heads. "Oh, for God's sake, stop with the posturing already. Mez, please tell Kai exactly why you've been doing what you've been doing before it's all too late."

Mez shook her head. "Kai never listens to anything that I have to say. He wouldn't begin to understand."

"Try me," Kai said, "make me understand. If there's one thing I'm sure about it's that this person isn't really who you are. What turned you this way?"

"Only if you promise not to interrupt, like you always-"

"I don't interrupt!"

"See, you just did!" Mez turned to look at me, "Can't you see, AJ, there really is no point, he-"

Whether it was *my/our* newly-found powers, or just the look of sheer exasperation on the face of *blue-me* I don't know but Mez suddenly turned and began to tell Kai everything that she knew about the Greville family.

Mez left no detail out, explaining how not only had she had been carrying out the attacks to hurt them financially, but how she'd also dug much deeper, investigating their finances and business connections. In return, Kai just stood and quietly listened, no doubt as astonished as *I/we* were at how the Grevilles had woven a their huge web of deceit and deception around the town, building their own power and wealth by profiting out of the misfortune of others. If hearing how loans and mortgages were sold at extortionate rates, families being left homeless, as Mez's parents were, when they couldn't keep up with the repayments wasn't proof enough, Mez's final revelation helped convince Kai that there might be some merit to her claims.

"And if that doesn't to convince you who the real villains are here," Mez sighed having reached the end of her impassioned speech, "then ask yourself this one final question. Why has no one ever really tried to clean up our streets before you?"

Kai stood silently for a moment before finally shrugging. "You tell me, Mez."

"It's because those on the streets late at night are

making too much money for their masters," Mez replied, adding, "and what better way to launder that money than by running it through their own bank." Kai closed his eyes momentarily before looking at *me/us*.

"What do you think, AJ – both of you!"

"You have to admit, it all makes a whole lot of sense," *I/we* replied, "for a city the size of Meggerlithick, we have far more poverty, social deprevation and inequality than other major cities in England. It can't just be a coincidence that ours is the only one where one family is so dominant Meggerlithick's affairs and the way that the city is run."

"So, what do you say, Kai," Mez asked, "can you put you principles aside just this once, please?"

"Only if you honestly answer me this," Kai replied, "what do you plan to do with all the money, valuables and property you've already stolen?"

"Oh, don't you worry about that," Mez said, "I already made plans as to what good I'm going to do with it once the time is right!"

Mez first looked at Kai, then *me/us* hopefully before he finally replied.

"OK, if it helps someone that the Grevilles have wronged, then I'll step aside."

"Thank you!" Mez replied, kissing Kai on the cheek before running to the door which led down from the roof top, "I won't be long, promise. I'll grab the bank note then we'll get out of here."

She was just about to open it when Kai spoke again.

"Mez?"

"Yes, Kai?"

"You know that this won't stop them, don't you?"
Mez bowed her head before nodding. "Yes, but it'll
give them a bloody nose for a bit."
"And then what?"
Mez frowned. "What do you mean?"
Kai sighed. "They'll come after you – and me – even
harder. What you are doing will irritate them yes, but
it won't stop then. They've too much money and
power behind them. They'll use all the resources at
their disposal to hunt us down."
Mez swallowed hard and smiled. "Then we'll just
have to lay low under the dust settles. They'll forget
about us after a while.
Kai went to reply but *I/we* cut across him.
"No they won't Mez, they'll never stop. You've
pulled the tail on the tiger and the Grevilles will hunt
you down until they devour both you and your loved
ones whole."
Mez and Kai looked at one another as, overhead, we
could hear the sound of a helicopter fast approaching.
"So, what do you suggest we do?" Mez asked, a little
desperation now filling her voice for the very first
time.
*I/we* smiled at both of them. "Don't worry, I have a
cunning plan. One that if we get it absolutely right,
will put paid to the Grevilles' grip on the city, as well
as ending the careers of Mesmerise and The
Wardrobe forever. And this is how we do it…"

# Chapter 15

Half an hour…

Thirty minutes…

One thousand, eight hundred seconds…

An episode of one of those dreary soap operas that seem less important or relevant since our world changed because of the first pandemic of the 21$^{st}$ century…

That's how long the *blue-me* stood waiting on the roof of the bank for Mez and Kai to return from their final missions as Mesmerise and The Wardrobe, hopefully enacting the plan that *I/we* had carefully detailed them.

They'd stood and listened in both awe and disbelief as *I/we* explained the detail behind it, smiles slowly beginning to fill their sceptical faces as they realised that were they to carry it out exactly as *I/we* suggested, then there could potentially be a way that all of us would be able to walk away from this whole situation without ever having to look over our shoulders for the Grevilles or the law again.

At first, they'd bombarded *me/us* with questions which *I/we* were able to bat away effortlessly before finally asking *me/us* how and when *I/we* had formulated such a simple but ingenious plan…

That was a question that *I/we* couldn't answer before sending them off, back into the building.

Even now, as *I/we* awaited their safe and, hopefully, successful return, *I/we* were unable to answer it for *myself/ourselves.*

It had just come to *me/us*, like everything had over the past few weeks.

The insights into *my/our* friends behaviour.

The dreams which, as it now transpired, were not dreams but a foreshadowing of future events, finally culminating into *me/us* evolving into whatever *I/we* were now.

*But there's no time for us to dwell on this now,* we thought to ourselves, choosing to identify the two forms as me in the plural sense, *we need to get out of here and soon.*

*"God, we sound like Sméagol and Gollum!" I/we* laughed as *I/we* glanced over the edge of the roof. Below the roof-top, a hive of activity was underway as *I/we* watched various search teams with sniffer dogs return to the buildings, their lead officers shaking their heads at those who were obviously in charge, coordinating the extensive hunt for the three of us through the streets of Meggerlithick.

*I/we* watched as *I/we* saw an officer in a peaked cap walk towards one of the police vehicles, reaching in to it before producing a loudhailer from deep within the confines of the white van.

"Ladies and Gentlemen," the officer boomed at the hordes of people, along with the camera men and film crews who were tightly packed around the perimeter of the cordon that had been put in place.

"Please may we ask you to move back. Our search of the area has proved fruitless, which means that the suspects have either escaped and are no longer in the vicinity…"

Even with *my/our* discovered powers, *I/we* knew exactly what the officer was about to say next.

"Or they have somehow doubled back and are at this very moment hiding out somewhere deep within the

First Bank of Meggerlithick."

*Come on guys, what's taking you so long, I/we* thought to ourselves, trying to search within the building for Mez and Kai, but sensing no trace of them.

Down below, two heavily armoured police teams holding Perspex shields and long nightsticks stood poised to storm the building, the remaining police officers standing along the edge of the cordon, forming a human shield, ready to stop anyone trying to break through it to steal an exclusive photo or to video the events first hand.

Above *me/us,* the buzzing sound of a helicopter grew nearer, a large beam of light now being shone on the building, causing *I/me* to hide by the side of the exit which led down into the bank.

However, *I/we* knew that it would only be a matter of time before the helicopter swept around to make out *my/our* blue form crouched in the shadows.

"Come on out with your hands held high in the air," the voice through the loudhailer below boomed, "we know that you're in there. Give yourselves up now or else we're coming in to get you."

*This is taking too long, I/we* thought, *they should have been out of there by now, something's gone terribly...* But before *I/we* could complete the thought, there was a loud *boom*, the bank shuddering beneath me as every single light or electrical device in the building either went out or stopped working, the electrical hum of the generators near *me/us* on the rooftop suddenly silenced.

*I/we* looked over the edge of the building and saw dozens of people drop the mobile phones, cameras, microphones or video cameras that they held onto the ground, each seemingly too hot to hold.

Only the helicopter high above *my/our* heads had seemed to have escaped whatever fate had befallen the equipment in and around the First Bank of Meggerlithick.

The helicopter now began to circle the building as *I/we* scurried around the exit from the roof, trying to avoid its beam which was sweeping every inch of the rooftop.

Just when it seemed that they would capture the *blue-me* in its white-light glare, the door to the roof burst open and Mesmerise and The Wardrobe stood there, hand in hand, causing the helicopter to swoop round behind them.

"Where are you?" Mesmerise shouted, trying to make herself heard above the droning sound of the helicopter's rotating blades as the two of them turned, momentarily blinded by the beam of its lights.

"Right here!" *I/we* shouted, walking out from where *I/we* hid to where they now stood, extending *my/our* hands towards them, "Are *we* glad to see you or what? You took your time though."

"Sorry about that," The Wardrobe replied, taking a blue hand, "it was a lot harder to find than we first thought."

"But you did find it?"

"Yep," Mesmerise replied, her eyes smiling through the view piece in her helmet as she took my other hand, "and we did exactly as you said. It worked like a dream! I'm still buzzing now…literally!"

"Were you seen?"

Kai laughed. "Oh, most definitely. We put on quite a

show, even if I do say so myself!"
Now the helicopter was rapidly circling us, so *I/we* bowed *my/our* heads, careful to ensure that the helicopter's crew could not make out *my/our* face. Fortunately, due to the age and style of the building, there was no safe way for it to land and, as yet, they showed no signs that they had any capability to land any of their occupants on the roof with us. Nevertheless, *I/we* didn't want to linger there any longer and tempt fate.
"Time to go, *we* think!" *I/we* said, gripping their hands tightly, "Ready?"
"Absolutely," Kai replied, closing his eyes.
"So how's this work then?" Mez said, copying her friend's actions.
"*We* have absolutely no idea!" *I/we* replied, closing my eyes, "*We've* never done this before…"

"AJ…AJ…are you all right?"
I was suddenly very aware of being shaken, a heavy pressure on both of my shoulders as I was rocked back and forth into consciousness.
"I'm, so sorry, AJ, please wake up!" the voice said, one that I slowly recognised as I opened my eyes to look into my mum's anxious face.
"Oh, hi Mum!" I smiled, "What's up?"
"Oh, for goodness sake, you scared the damned life out of me," Mum replied curtly, stepping away as she stood up to look at me, still sat on the side of my bed as I was before.
I looked around, suddenly very aware that there was only one of me – the *bedroom-me,* still sat in exactly the same position I was when I'd *multi-tasked* to be

with Mez and Kai.

*Mez and Kai,* I anxiously thought, suddenly recalling my last moments with them.

Or had I dreamt it all?

Fear began to overtake me again, my chest tightening and my heart racing at the thought that I had somehow created the last hour or so in my mind.

And just in my mind alone.

But before I could dwell on it any longer, my mum spoke once again.

"You really had me worried there for a moment or two," she sighed though her anger had began to dissipate slightly, "though it was my own stupid fault."

My brain was still foggy and fuzzy, trying to make sense as to what was real or not anymore.

"What was your fault, Mum? I'm sorry, I'm just a little bit muddled and confused as to what you're on about."

Mum smiled and sat on the bed next to me, gently taking my hand. "That's because of the bang on your head, *serduszko*, don't you remember?"

"Oh, that…" I replied, touching the bump which now threatened to split the skin on my forehead, "Yes, of course I do."

"Good, good," Mum smiled, standing, "I was worried that you'd fallen asleep as the hospital said not to let you for a little while until we were sure that you were OK."

"I wasn't asleep, Mum, at least I don't think I was," I smiled, hoping that she would soon leave the room so that I could check the phone I still held in my hand to see if I'd had a reply to the messages I'd sent my friends earlier.

I was desperate to know whether everything that had happened over the past couple of hours or so was real or just a figment of my imagination, a result of the concussion I'd suffered earlier that day.

Fortunately, Mum helped to ease my fears without even realising it as she kissed my forehead and went to leave the room.

"I'd have never forgiven myself had anything happened to you," she smiled, "serves me right from not checking on you though. Became so engrossed with what's been going on that I clean forgot that you were home upstairs!"

"What do you mean, *'what's been going on?'*" I asked, hope now beginning to glow in my heart.

"Don't you know?" Mum said, before shaking her head and laughing, "No, of course you don't! Those scoundrels Mesmerise and The Wardrobe launched an attack on the First Bank of Meggerlithick. It's been all over the news these past couple of hours. Come downstairs and I'll tell you all about."

"Will do," I smiled, relief seeping out of every pore in my body, "just give me a minute to sort myself out, Mum."

I waited until she had left the room before I entered my passcode and tapped the messages icon on my phone.

Suddenly, I began to laugh loudly, tears welling up in my eyes as I gazed at the screen.

There was the last message *bedroom-me* had sent my friends.

ME: My 2 BFFs, standin beside each
other opposite a red-haired
smurf on the roof of the bank
wondering how the hell we get
ourselves out of this mess...

But now, below it, were two, new replies...
Both of them telling me that all was well with the
world again...

KAI: Home! I don't know how you
did it, but I'm damned glad you did!
Thanks AJ, owe you one! 😊

I smiled at the second longest message that Kai had
ever sent me before reading the next message...

MEZ: Whoah! Wot a ride! Don't
know bout u but I can't wait 2 c
wot old Sherman-baby has
2 say 2 nite! 😜 💚

# Chapter 16

The rest of the day, until Dad came home from work that is, I spent sat on the couch in the lounge, being showered with tea and sympathy by my mum as I flicked through the various national and local TV channels and news stations, watching, listening to what was being said about the events that morning at the First Bank of Meggerlithick.

It was quite something to see us make the national stations, though they were only reporting what our local news teams had already previously shown, Meggerlithick not normally being considered a city where anything newsworthy ever happened.

But now, on the screen before me, were the shops me and my friends used, the High Street we regularly walked down and the rubber-necking locals who were desperate to get onto any live news feed or outside broadcast link made with the multitude of reporters who were now at the scene, feeding back snippets of information, gleaming whatever they could from them.

Dad had been the most animated I had seen him in ages as he and Mum chatted about what he'd heard on the radio and what we'd seen on the TV whilst we waited for our dinner to cook.

But they, like the rest of the people who lived in and around Meggerlithick knew that there was only one place to go if you wanted to find out exactly what had happened in our city that day (those of us who weren't actually there of course).

*Go West*.

And, sure enough, having sat with Mum and Dad,

eating our dinner off our laps whilst the national news had barely paid lip-service to the biggest news story to hit Meggerlithick in decades, preferring to concentrate on the antics of our buffoon of a Prime Minister instead, the three of us settled back into our seats to watch the local legend that was Sherman Dibnah.

"And in a change to our advertised schedule," Voice-over Man announced over the latest ident for BBC Wessex, "we now cross live to Sherman Dibnah for a specially extended edition of *Go West*."

"Oh I wonder if he's wearing the black suit, Stefan," Mum said excitedly, "he always wears the black suit when it's something serious. God, I *love* him in that black suit!"

"Shush, Mum, I'm trying to listen!" I said, leaning forward in my seat, causing my dad to chuckle to himself.

"Tonight, *Go West* comes live to you from the streets of Meggerlithick," Sherman Dibnah, in his crisp back suit, said sombrely, "as its community comes to terms with the shocking events that have unfolded there today."

The screen changed, showing a series of clips, reports and interviews that we had watched throughout the course of the day on the various channels and stations that me and my mum had surfed.

Mum sat back in her chair and smiled contently as Sherman Dibnah's narrative recapped the day's main events day, repeating everything that had already been broadcast, analysed and dissected by all of the other media outlets that had descended on our city in the hours since the three of us had made our dramatic and spectacular escape.

"Oh, turn it off, Stefan," Mum said, "as much as I like a good ogle of old Sherman, there's nothing here that we don't already know. Switch the channel over and let's find something that's a little more cheery instead.

For once, neither me or my dad put up much of an argument as Dad got up to fetch the remote control. But, as though seeing him rise out of his armchair, Sherman Dibnah suddenly reappeared on screen, holding what looked like a DVD in his hand.

"Hold on a second, Dad," I said, "this might be interesting."

Sure enough, what Sherman Dibnah next said had me and my parents glued to our sets for the rest of the programme...

"But tonight, dear viewer," Sherman Dibnah said gravely, "*Go West* can exclusively reveal, through sources close to the investigation, exactly what happened *inside* the First Bank of Meggerlithick this morning, as well as showing you the final moments of the supervillains known as Mesmerise and The Wardrobe, along with another, unknown and unnamed Smurf-like figure as they all simply vanished into thin air..."

*At last,* I thought to myself as Sherman Dibnah's voice continued, only this time commentating on the grainy black and white footage that was now being shown on the screen.

"First we see the supervillain Mesmerise swiping the million-pound note which was the centre-piece of the exhibition, taking advantage of the confusion that she and The Wardrobe had caused to occur outside of the bank, " Sherman Dibnah said gravely as I watched Mesmerise casually lift the lid on the glass case that the note was hidden under.

I struggled to contain my laughter as Mesmerise turned toward the CCTV camera and waved the note at it before tucking it into her jacket pocket as she ran up the stairs.

"Note that at this stage, there is no sign of her accomplice, The Wardrobe," said Sherman Dibnah, "though it wasn't long before he made an appearance, confirming his part in this audacious attack on the bank."

Now the scene changed, as though a channel had been turned over, the screen now showing a long corridor. At one end were the top of a flight of stairs which ended beside a heavily secured, thick steel door.

"We next catch sight of Mesmerise here on the third floor," Sherman Dibnah continued, "no doubt looking to make her escape from the building up onto the rooftop above. Watch now as The Wardrobe breaks cover to greet her."

"See! Didn't I tell you that he was a wrong one," Mum smugly declared.

Dad and I turned and shot her a look.

"I know," Mum smiled, "Shush! You're both trying to watch the programme."

By now the screen was filled with the grainy image of Mesmerise and The Wardrobe stood in the centre of the corridor, right next to the heavy, steel door.

"However," Sherman Dibnah announced, "observe how things seem to get a little heated between the two accomplices."

*And the award for Best Actress goes to Mez Monroe,*
I smiled to myself as I watched her silently and
theatrically begin to gesticulate toward The
Wardrobe, each movement she made wildly
exaggerated, as though she were a star of the silent
cinema, putting on exactly the performance I'd hoped
that she would in order to sell our lie to the viewing
public.

In fairness, Kai more than held his own, puffing his
chest out as he waved a clenched fist at Mesmerise,
suddenly sweeping his hand before him as though
demanding she put the million-pound note back.

This apparent fact wasn't lost on Sherman Dibnah
who continued to speculate on the CCTV footage that
the producers of *Go West* had spliced together,
desperate to steal both a march on, and the ratings of,
their numerous tea-time competitors.

"But now witness, dear viewer, how our two
protagonists appear to have an extremely bitter and
heated argument in this shot," the voice-over
continued sagely, "could it be that The Wardrobe had
a sudden crisis of conscience and was actually was
trying to stop Mesmerise? Or was he hoping to cut
her out of their ill-gotten gains?"

*Oh this is solid gold-dust,"* I smiled as I watched The
Wardrobe grab and lift Mesmerise, throwing her the
entire length of the corridor.

However, by the way that she landed, I could tell that
the two of them must have been talking each other
through their staged fight, Mez using her former
gymnastic skills to good effect.

"No doubt, shocked by her accomplice's betrayal,
Mesmerise then strikes back herself, using her

mesmeric power to force The Wardrobe back…"
Now, Mez had placed her hand to the side of her
head, bowing it slightly as she began to walk forward.
By contrast, The Wardrobe was now moving
backward at the same rate – courtesy of Kai's
cleverly disguised moonwalk skills – making it
appear that Mesmerise were forcing him back with
her mind alone, Kai eventually falling to the floor.
At this point, I had to sit on my hands for fear that I
would accidentally applaud their efforts, so brilliantly
were they telling the elaborate story that I had
somehow concocted out of thin air.
*Now for the finishing touch,* I thought as, suddenly,
Mesmerise stood bolt upright and thrust her hand
forward, the gesture clearly indicating 'Stop!' for
anyone watching.
"What happens next is truly remarkable," Sherman
Dibnah whispered breathlessly as Mesmerise reached
inside her jacket pocket and retrieved the hastily
scribbled sheet of paper that we had written together
before they had left the roof earlier, thrusting it at The
Wardrobe, who theatrically snatched it from her
hands and began to read it, his head moving slowly
back and forth across the page.
"Whatever the note said, there is no doubt that it
ultimately determined the fates of both Mesmerise
and The Wardrobe," Sherman Dibnah announced
over the image of Mez helping Kai to his feet.
Slowly, The Wardrobe began to nod his head, which
caused Mesmerise to throw her arms around him.
"It was at this moment that what had started out as
just the simple theft of a rare banknote turned into
something more cataclysmic for the First Bank of

Meggerlithick," Sherman Dibnah whispered as The Wardrobe wrapped his arms around Mesmerise in return.

At this point, as I had somehow known and predicted, the raw, extraordinary powers that both my friends possessed, those that had originally forced them apart, now drew them together, generating an electromagnetic pulse that wiped out every electrical and electronic device in a 500 metre radius of it.

"Not only did their embrace fry mobile phones as well as the television cameras that gathered on the streets below," Sherman Dibnah explained, "but it also destroyed all electrical and electronic for a couple of blocks, the worst casualty being the mainframe computer system of the First Bank of Meggerlithick, deleting its cloud backups in the process."

"Couldn't they just turn it on and off again?" Mum asked.

"It's not as easy as that, love," Dad replied, "if it was an electromagnetic pulse, it will have wiped anything and everything on it, meaning that all of the bank's files and records would be lost forever."

I smiled to myself, secretly hoping that Dad was right and that the first part of my plan had succeeded, knowing that there was soon to be an additional twist in the tale to follow.

Sherman Dibnah reappeared on screen, confirming what Dad had told my Mum, explaining that according to sources, the data lost could cost the bank millions as the Greville family would have no idea as to which families and businesses owed them what.

"Additionally," Sherman Dibnah added, "all records

of outstanding mortgages could have been lost too."

"What does that mean, Stefan?" Mum asked

A huge smile broke out on Dad's face. "It would mean that this house is ours as technically the bank would have no idea what we owed them. Heck, they probably wouldn't be able to find any records that they even leant us the money in the first place!"

Mum went to answer, but the images now being shown, accompanied by Sherman Dibnah's continued commentary silenced our living room.

"Now, another *Go West* exclusive!" the presenter said dramatically, "we have gained access to the final moments of today's attack on the bank by way of live footage obtained from the dashcam of the police helicopter which witnessed the disappearance of Mesmerise and The Wardrobe, along with an unidentified third, mysterious accomplice."

Goosebumps rippled across every square inch of my body, partly out of anticipation at seeing what the *blue-me* actually looked like on camera.

But that excitement was also tempered by the fear that I would somehow be recognised as I was the only one of the three of us not wearing a mask that morning on the roof.

It didn't help that I was sitting watching the debut of a third, previously unknown superhuman with the two people in the whole world who knew me the best, knowing every awkward movement I now made as a gawky teenager.

Fortunately, I needn't have worried as the footage shown was shot from behind, capturing the moment that Mez and Kai joined me on the roof just before I stepped out of the shadows and approached them with both hands outstretched towards them.

"Unfortunately," Sherman Dibnah's disappointed voiceover continued to explain to the viewer, "this mysterious figure's face remains unseen by the police camera. But we can clearly see that he or she has unnaturally looking red hair – almost volcanic red – as well as the skin visible on its arms, ears and back of the neck being the most vivid of blues..."

*Not bad,* I thought, thinking that my skin and hair resembled one of the more popular characters out of Marvel's X-Men comics.

However, this heroic image I imagined as was soon destroyed by my mum, who announced that when looking at '*that hideous, unnatural looking creature*' she was reminded of one of the *My Little Ponies* that she collected when she was younger.

"I'm sure its name was Paradise Pony or something cute, unlike that...that...*thing*!" Mum said.

"You sure it wasn't Psycho-Papa Smurf Pony!" Dad scoffed, nudging me in the side, encouraging me to laugh at his lame joke.

*Not you as well, Dad,* I thought as I faked a chuckle at my mum's expense.

Before Mum could respond, Sherman Dibnah's voice became more animated again.

"...suddenly, the three supervillains grabbed each other's hands and simply vanished into thin air!"

The three of us watched intently as Mez, Kai and myself disappeared, the spaces that we had occupied just moments before seeming to shimmer as though we'd simply been erased from existence, the only sign that we had ever been there being a solitary piece of paper which fluttered down to the roof of the building.

"Goodbye to bad rubbish!" Mum said, clapping her hands, "Let's hope that's the last we see of any superhumans around here anytime soon!"

*Don't worry, Mum,* I thought, *if all goes to plan, you'll never see any of our alter-egos again.*

"True," Dad said, reaching for the remote control, changing the channel to the football, "but they could have accidentally made a lot of Meggerlithick very happy and better off tonight by what those superhumans have done."

I smiled to myself as Dad settled back into his seat, Mum picking up her knitting again as my phone buzzed not once, but twice in my pocket.

There was no need for my newly-discovered foresight as I unlocked my phone.

I knew exactly who the texts would be from, as well as having a pretty good idea as to what they would both say....

**KAI: Hey AJ! Looks like they bought It. Part one complete!**

**MEZ: Wow! We rocked, didn't we AJ? I wonder wots gonna happen nxt...?😊 Can't w8! L8rs x**

*Me neither,* I thought as I settled back into my seat and enjoyed my first, super-friend-free, worry-free night in months, knowing that if everything went to plan, our superhero days were over forever...

# Chapter 17

That was a little under a year ago.
Mez, Kai and myself have kept a very low profile
since then, the search for us Supers having been
scaled back considerably by the police and other
agencies keen to capture and interview us, no doubt a
few official and unofficial government ones being
included in that select group.
At first, in the days and weeks that followed our
dramatic escape, there were regular newspaper
articles, news reports and public appeals for
information about our whereabouts, along with plenty
of rumours, stories, whispers, false sightings and
alleged eye-witness accounts of seeing one or all of
us after our roof top disappearance...
*'Mesmerise Mesmerised My Mum!'* was one fanciful
headline, whilst *'Coming Out of Closet: The Secret
Life of The Wardrobe'* was an exclusive 'secret'
account written by the elusive superhero himself...
Allegedly.
Of course, it wasn't, it being just another of the
dozens of fake news stories created by a media who
were still desperately trying to cash in on our
celebrity to boost flagging ratings and circulations.
My own, personal favourite from this time was the
tabloid headline *'Super Surfing Smurf Saved My
Sister!'* claiming that *blue-me* had performed a
Baywatch-type rescue from under the pier in Weston-
Super-Mare.
*I'm good*, I thought as I watched the report on
television that night, *but even I would have had
difficulty being in three places at once - blue-me*

staying at home doing my homework that weekend whilst *bedroom-me* was at the funfair with Mez and Kai!

However, things started to improve for us, and for the city on the whole, when the police, having employed additional manpower in their hunt for us, started to turn their attentions to the note found on the roof of the First Bank of Meggerlithick.

The note that we had carefully written together...

The note detailing all the allegations that Mesmerise had made against the Greville family...

The note containing all of the information Mez had to back up her claims...

The note Mesmerise *accidentally* dropped...

The note that somehow ended up in the hands of Sherman Dibnah, who read it out, live-on-air, on *Go West* one night soon after, saying that he'd received it from *'an unnamed source'*, following it up the night after with one of those interviews where you can't see the person's face, them being filmed from behind by the television camera, their words spoken by an actor instead to protect their identity.

Whoever the mole was in the Greville organisation we may never know, but they helped confirm a lot of the accusations that had been made against them.

When I asked Dad what he thought about all the tip-offs and secret information that had somehow been leaked to the programme in the weeks after the attack on the bank, asking him why they had never come out before the Supers had made their claims, he told me that it was probably someone extremely close to the Grevilles who'd been too afraid to ever speak up before about what they either knew or suspected.

"But, perhaps, they finally gained the courage to speak out after what they saw Mesmerise and The Wardrobe do at the bank that day," Dad said, adding, "and if they then were the one who found and read the note themselves, it might have encouraged them to step forward to help finish off what the Supers have started."

That made me smile.

It's not often that kids show adults the way, let alone help someone else to become their own kind of superhero, encouraging them to speak out, hoping to help the people of Meggerlithick to be rid of the corrupt and evil stranglehold that the Grevilles had had on the city for centuries.

Sherman Dibnah's expose had an instant and immediate effect, with the mayor being forced to resign, under much protest of his innocence, the very next day.

The police's attention then focused on investigating the Grevilles and their extensive list of business and political associates.

Unfortunately, many of the files needed to prove their guilt beyond question the electromagnetic pulse had obliterated but enough doubt had been cast their way that businesses and organisations connected to, and associated with them suffered as a result as people stopped using them or transferred their affairs elsewhere.

It meant that the police department, freed from the mayor's control and vice-like grip, having themselves been emboldened by the Supers, as well as being cheered on by a public thirsty for blood, swept through the city, cleaning up the alleys and the streets, arresting dozens of criminals, thereby disbanding and destroying the organised crime syndicates who had ruled the night for many a long year.

Eventually, Meggerlithick had once more become a more happy, hopeful and prosperous place as hundreds of families now venturing back into its city centre, with more outward investment flooding into the local economy as a whole host of new bars, restaurants and entertainment venues opened up in and around Meggerlithick.

Now the city was back on the map for all the right reasons, *'the hippest and wildest city in the west,' Sherman* Dibnah quipped at the end of *Go West* one night.

At last, teenagers and young adults didn't have to wish their lives away, desperately waiting until they were of an age when they could leave Meggerlithick, moving away to live in far more popular, trendier and more prosperous cities, leaving their heartbroken families behind them.

Now we all had futures which we could dream of and shape ourselves, our world an empty canvas once again…

And as for the three of us - well we're still besties of course, though the dynamic has changed slightly.

Mez and Kai are now *a thing*, having pretty much dated ever since hugging one another on the third floor of the bank.

Mind you, if you ask me, they'd always been building toward that moment, it just needed something to give them a jolt, a push in the right direction.

And what better way to do that than a super-charged-electromagnetic pulse to help draw two perfect people together.

When my mum found out, she said that she'd give them *'three weeks at the most'* and to make sure that I could still be friends with both of them *'when they inevitably break up.'*

I asked her if she wanted to place a bet on that as I thought that they'd be together a lot longer than that.

Foolishly, she took the bet at twenty pounds for every year they were to stay together...

I'm looking forward to soon claiming the first twenty and then all the others that will undoubtably follow.

If only she knew that there are some things that I already know about the future, such as the fact that Mez and Kai are set for a very long and happy life together...

Like me, they've been careful not to use their powers so as to not alert anyone as to who they really are.

But, let's face it, we're all only fifteen or therabouts, so we can't be perfect all the time!

There's been the odd lapse...or two...or three!

However, like me, we tend to only use our superpowers in very small doses and normally it's just for our own purposes.

For example, Kai has been scouted by several professional football teams, their scouts and coaches impressed by the strength he possesses when holding the ball against much larger opponents.

And as for his pace...

'Explosive,' one seasoned scout had commented when offering him signing on forms.

*If only they knew...*

Mez, on the other hand, has been content to let a little

of her talent out every single day, charming all that she meets spreading a little sunshine into their lives everywhere she goes.

I like this new-found peace and contentment in her, Mez's homelife having improved dramatically as her mother has been able to get back on her feet again, all of the debt that she'd been struggling with now wiped from existence.

Mez even kept it together when Geoff eventually moved in, though she did somehow manage to persuade him to lose the beard before he did so…

She's also been true to her word regarding all of the proceeds of the raids that she'd carried out, various charities and social projects receiving *'mysterious donations from an unnamed source'* helping hundreds of people, ranging from the homeless to those who had previously had regularly use the city's foodbanks just to survive from one week to the week.

And me?

Well, most of the time I'm just that – me!

Only occasionally, as when the funfair was in town, do I choose to be in two places at once, but these are very few and far between.

You see, blue isn't really my colour…

But it's a handy gift to have should I ever need to use it to help my family or friends if they're in trouble, or there's an emergency in the future.

The funny thing is, just *knowing* I have this gift has made my far more confident and assured in myself, something I'd have never believed possible when simply acting as a go-between, keeping my friends' secrets safe, secrets like no other.

All told, things have worked out for the best and I

inally feel really happy, positive and excited for the future.

I've a feeling that it's going to be a great one...

Pretty super, in fact...

Also by Jonas Lane

*Slipp In Time*
*Slipp, Sliding Away*
*Nona's Ark*
*Dragonchasers*
*Another Time, Slipp!*
*Grammarticus*
*Poppy Copperthwaite*
*Tall, Dark*
*and Twisted Tales*

Also by Jonas Lane's
Young Writers

# *Write Here…Write Now!*
# *Bonechillers*
# *Magic, Mischief and Mayhem*
# *Scary Stories*
# *Timeslipping*
# *Spellbound*
# *Out of this World*
# *Timehunters*

All book titles available to purchase from
www.JonasLaneAuthor.com
or by ordering from amazon.co.uk

# Slipp In Time

Living in the sleepy village of Codswallop, adventure-hungry Alex McClellan and his cousin want nothing more than for something, anything, exciting to happen to them. More often than not, however, they end up disappointed.

Then one quiet Saturday, whilst delivering newspapers, they meet the eccentric Lord Thyme-Slipp, who tells them tall-tales about his inventions, including his very own time machine. Despite being given a brief time-trip, they remain unconvinced and return home to find things to do to stop them being more bored than usual.

As they are playing on the computer, fate intervenes. They realise that their only hope in undoing the damage that they have done is to put their trust and belief in the kindly old man and travel back just a few hours in time. But a raging storm and a nervous cat propel them hundreds of years into the past, back to a far simpler time and place in history, causing yet more chaos on their arrival.

There they face a race against time to sort out the mess that they have created, before trying to find their way back home again...

# Slipp Sliding Away!

Slipp, Alex and Georgie are back! Literally!
Our misadventurers are back in the present day. But home is a whole different world now from the one that they left less than twenty-four hours before.
Returning to school after the summer holidays, Alex and Georgie are shocked to find that all that they once believed is no more, replaced by an alternative history dominated by a name from the past, of a man that they had briefly encountered before.

Discovering that they may be directly responsible for this strange, new world, the children have no choice but to ask again for help from their kind, but eccentric, inventor friend to right the wrongs caused by their actions. Using his not-so-technical no-how, Slipp has now modified the Time Skipper to help take them back to the exact time and place in the past where fate intervened to change the future.
But a careless mistake and a simple coincidence disrupts their plans as they find themselves pitched into the middle of a deadly argument between two powerful and ambitious men who hold the fate of a kingdom in their hands...

*Slipp Sliding Away* is the highly anticipated sequel to the acclaimed debut novel, *Slipp In Time*. Building on a world where fun, action and adventure sit alongside nonsense, history and time-travel, Jonas Lane has plunged his characters back into a long-lost time once again that will engage and educate readers of all ages, old and new.

# Nona's Ark

Twelve-year-old Nona Lancaster thought that her life was finally on the up, having moved to the school of her dreams where she got to spend her entire day playing sports with her best friends.

However, a sudden, final unexpected and unwanted gift from her secret grandfather soon turned her life on its head.

Faced with a desperate race against time to thwart her new brother's evil plans for the zoo that she too now owned, Nona and her friends embark on the adventure of a lifetime to rescue the animals her grandfather had devoted his life to...

A madcap story in the style of the 1950s Ealing Comedies featuring school children, wild animals and an eccentric head teacher, *Nona's Ark* is an adventure for all ages!

# Dragonchasers:
## Book 1 – The Knight School

A group of gifted youngsters presented with the chance of a lifetime when offered the opportunity of a free scholarship at one of England's finest, but most elusive, schools.

An ancient evil hiding amongst us, having watched, and plotted our demise for thousands of years, waiting for the moment to strike again.

A secret society tasked with defending humankind, protecting us from a legendary enemy who seeks to return from the shadows and reclaim a world they believe to be rightfully theirs once more.

Part Harry Potter.
Part Da Vinci Code.
All action and adventure, *The Knight School* is the first, gripping adventure in the Dragonchasers series.

*Here be dragons...*

# Another Time, Slipp!

Slipp is back, way, way back!

Having escaped just in the nick of time before the bloody battle of Hastings, Slipp, Alex and Georgie find that they are, yet again, far from home and lost somewhere in time.

Stranded in an England greatly suspicious of strangers, recovering from an attack by one of the nation's deadliest rivals, our misadventurers find themselves pitched into a war of words between two of history's most famous and finest heroes and adventurers.

Faced with finding a way to escape the past, as well as fixing a misguided attempt to correct the future, our terrible trio yet again bumble their way through a past-world where words speak louder than actions...

The third Lord Thyme-Slipp adventure, *Another Time, Slipp* picks up exactly where it last left off, catapulting the reader into a pivotal period in English history in this thrill-a-page adventure which excites, entertains and informs in equal measures.

# Grammarticus

Mind your language...
Watch what you say...
The pen is mightier than the sword and more deadly!

When a small group of school friends, faced with the prospect of failing their impending SATs tests, stumble across an old and mysterious grammar book, they think that their prayers have finally been answered.

Instead, Grammarticus poses them more questions than answers, setting them on a deadly collision course with an evil teacher intent on using the book and its secrets for herself...

Grammarticus is the latest, exciting adventure, full of magic, mischief and mayhem from the pen of Jonas Lane.

# Poppy Copperthwaite

Born into a magical ethnic community, on her 18th birthday Poppy Copperthwaite expected to receive the keys to her parents' kingdom at her *Coming of Mage* ceremony, a day for all Majeeks to celebrate her being recognised as their future leader.

However, the cruel hand of fate conspires against Poppy, causing her family's greatest rivals to doubt her claim to the throne in front of millions.

Poppy's parents are forced to seek medical and magical help, sending her to the private Majeek health and well-being farm known as the Foundation for Unleashing the Natural Numinous of Youth.

There, accompanied by her loyal but wildly unpredictable servant Humphry, Poppy undertakes a series of tests and tasks to determine what magical powers – if any – she actually possesses, under the watchful eye of Doctor Leopold Harryhausen.

However, with the clock counting down the days before she must prove that she is naturally born of Majeek blood, Poppy, Humphry and Harryhausen struggle to find a way to unlock the magical secrets hidden deep within her so that she can truly become the Spellcaster that she was always destined to be…

# Tall, Dark and Twisted Tales

From the pen of Jonas Lane comes a collection of tales, both old and new, which are sure to amuse and confuse, as well as sending tiny shivers of fear tingling down his readers' spines.

Gathered together for the very first time, *Tall, Dark and Twisted Tales* includes fourteen short stories, novelettes and teaser text which cross a range of different genres and writing style.

As well as those previously published to accompany his *Young Writers* series of anthologies, Jonas has also exclusively written several new pieces which are published here for the very first time.

For those of you new to the work of Jonas Lane, *Tall, Dark and Twisted Tales* will leave you wanting to explore the rest of his amazing world of writing even more…

# Praise from the readers of Jonas Lane's books

"As an avid reader, I know when I've found something special when I can't pull myself away from a book. I read Slipp In Time in only a few hours and loved every minute of it! I laughed, giggled, had to pause due to said giggling, and then I laughed some more. It's a brilliant story, and I highly recommend it for children and adults alike."

"Loved it! Great to read a kids' book that has pace adventure and humour. Having the main protagonists as a boy and a girl means that any child can identify with the story. What's not to like about time travel on a sofa! Watch out for 'Hamster Ragu' and 'pomegranate shootout'! As an English teacher, this is one I will definitely be reading with my students. Looking forward to the next one.... did I mention the tantalising cliffhanger at the end?"

"A really good adventure of two young children on a journey, including history and good humour. Kids will definitely enjoy this book and with a cliffhanger like that will be eagerly awaiting the next episode and adventure!"

"I bought this book for my 10-year-old daughter. Despite being an avid reader, she always chooses very similar reading styles (cute puppies, girls having sleepovers, blah blah!) Therefore, I wanted to help widen her reading world. Boy did this book fit the brief! Engaging characters and a writing style that made her want a second book immediately! Can't wait for the sequel!!"

"Excellent read from start to finish. Could not stop turning the pages once I started."

"… brilliant for children and teenagers that love an adventure."

"Fantastic book! Bought this for my 11-year-old son to encourage him to read… he loved it and can't wait for more!"

"I bought this for my 9-year-old daughter who loves anything to do with science and time travel! She absolutely loved it and read it in a couple of days. Well written and easy to comprehend and fitting with today's society. Bring on the next one!"

"Bought this book for myself...loved the imagination of the author...would recommend it to anyone who loves to read and put themselves into the story. Look forward to his and my next journey!"

"Fantastic…loved the story and the references to history. Can't wait for the next book to see what's happened. What a cliffhanger!"

"A fantastic read, suited for all ages, with relatable characters and an interesting plot. The book has a brilliant ending that has left me wanting the second instalment already!"

"Amazing and clever storyline that kept my 8-year-old daughter (and us!) hooked!! What a cliffhanger at the end! Cannot wait to read the next one and really hope there will be more. Excellent!!!"

"A very good read for children and adults. Includes time travel, humour and history. I will recommend this book and I think it'll encourage more children to read!"

"Great follow up, well worth the wait, my son loved it!"

"Bought this book for my seven-year-old son. He really enjoyed it, as did I! Believable characters, funny situations with good links to real events in history. We are both looking forward to the next Slipp story!"

"A lovely story, cleverly written. Once you start to read it you can't put it down. Great characters and plot make it seem perfect for a typical British film."

"Brilliant...This should be rated six stars!"

"Really enjoyed this, suitable for all ages, needs to be a film!"

"...most writers write in a similar way, but Jonas Lane doesn't...that's what makes his books unlike any others."
"My children are reluctant readers and this book has engaged both my children aged 9 and 13 to read, my youngest said this book is fun and exciting. My 13-year-old is dyslexic and has read very few books from cover to cover but he read all this one, so thank you for this book being accessible for all, looking forward to the next one."

"A fantastic read, suited for all ages, with relatable characters and an interesting plot. The book has a brilliant ending that has left me wanting the second instalment already!
"Captivating...Just finished reading this novel with my 6-year-old. We loved it and it had her gripped throughout. Loved how the ending left us wanting more. Fortunately, we have the second novel to hand ready to start straight away!

"A very good read for children and adults. Includes time travel, humour and history. I will recommend this book and I think it'll encourage more children to read."

"My teaching assistant bought the Slipp books and read them to my class during lunch. When we started a new genre – adventure stories – in English, my children were so inspired that they created their own time travel stories! These books really helped my class to develop their own characters and problems that they had to resolve. I would recommend this book to all teachers as I was able to help develop and then read stories that my class were very proud of writing."

"Fantastic story about 2 children on an adventure. Loved the story and the references to history. Can't wait for the next book to see what's happened. What a cliffhanger!"

"Fantastic easy read story for all ages, adventure and history all in one. Ends with a great cliffhanger can't wait for the next adventure."

"After reading the first book in this series, both my eldest daughter and I were desperate to get our hands on this next book! Once again Jonas Lane hasn't disappointed with his well-balanced mix of humour and history. The easy to read style of these brilliant books means that my youngest daughter now is wanting to join in. Hopefully, the next one is in the pipeline, so we can all have one each!!!!"

"Super sequel! Great book - my daughter loved it"

"A heartwarming story full of humour, excitement and morality. Written in a dynamic rhythm that keeps you willfully entranced!"

"Five Stars!"

Thanks to all those that have left such wonderful comments. Authors and writers live or die by the reviews given by their readers. Please take a moment to share your opinions and leave a review by visiting the site that you purchased this book from.

Alternatively, visit Jonas at his website as he would welcome your feedback.

**www.jonaslaneauthor.com**

Printed in Poland
by Amazon Fulfillment
Poland Sp. z o.o., Wrocław